"Why no
and stay here…?"

As he spoke Roland reached for her hand, and Carly realized he wasn't smiling. She had thought they'd agreed that any matchmaking was preposterous.

"Oh, Roland," she stammered, "I think you're one of the nicest men I know, but—oh, can't you see that the idea's crazy?"

Liam suddenly loomed over them as Roland replied, "So you said. But why?"

"Because…" Carly began desperately.

"Because," drawled Liam, "Carly and I are lovers. We've been together every night since she's been here. Which might not make her marrying you crazy—but it would make it something of a calculated risk."

Carly wanted to scream, but it came out as a croaking gasp. There seemed to be no end to the pain Liam was determined to inflict upon her.…

JANE DONNELLY
is also the author of these
Harlequin Romances

Many of these titles are available at your local bookseller.

For a free catalogue listing all available Harlequin Romances
and Harlequin Presents, send your name and address to:

HARLEQUIN READER SERVICE,
1440 South Priest Drive, Tempe, AZ 85281
Canadian address: Stratford, Ontario N5A 6W2

Flash Point

by

JANE DONNELLY

Harlequin Books

TORONTO · LONDON · LOS ANGELES · AMSTERDAM
SYDNEY · HAMBURG · PARIS · STOCKHOLM · ATHENS · TOKYO

Original hardcover edition published in 1981
by Mills & Boon Limited

ISBN 0-373-02456-8

Harlequin edition published February 1982

Printed in U.S.A.

CHAPTER ONE

'OH, my gosh!' murmured Carly Brown. She was on her knees in the window of the small boutique where she worked, arranging a dress so that it showed to best advantage, when she looked up and saw the old lady looking in with a tear trickling down her cheek. Then a shaking hand went up to cover her eyes and she seemed to Carly to be swaying.

Carly was out of the window and out of the shop in a flash, asking anxiously, 'Are you all right?'

The old lady must have been strikingly beautiful once. She was still beautiful, but now her pale skin looked paper-thin, and her voice sounded very old and very tired as she whispered, 'I'm sorry, I was just being rather silly.'

'Join the club,' said Carly. 'So am I, most of the time.' She smiled as she spoke, a light hand under the old lady's elbow, and the support of her strong young fingers, or the warmth of her concern, got a faint answering smile. 'Do come in and sit down for a few minutes,' she urged, 'and I'll get you a cup of tea.'

'Oh, I couldn't trouble you. I really am perfectly all right.' The old lady's voice had the crystal clear enunciation of a bygone age and a faint, faint trace of an accent Carly couldn't identify, and she was really smiling now, a composed and sweet smile. But Carly could feel her trembling, and said firmly, 'No bother at all. It's this beastly wind, it cuts through you.' There was a sharp east wind today, although it was still summer, and the old lady looked as though her blood was thin.

The shop was empty except for Ruth Clarkson, who owned it and who had been putting the Reductions rail back into size order when Carly shot past her. Carly was a girl who moved fast, given to acting at speed, but that dash had made Ruth jump and stare. She had seen Carly reach the old lady, speak to her, and now she was ushering her into the shop.

She didn't look like a customer, most of their clothes were young styles, and she didn't look well. Ruth got the message from Carly's expression and came to meet them.

'A cup of tea will be no trouble, will it?' said Carly, guiding her companion towards a bamboo armchair with a patchwork cushion, into which she sank down gratefully, murmuring,

'Oh, I am being a nuisance!'

'Not at all,' said Ruth.

'Honestly,' said Carly, 'we were going to have a cup of tea.' She went through to the little office and switched on the electric kettle, and the old lady sat very quiet and still, her hands in kid gloves folded on her lap. 'I thought she was going to faint,' Carly whispered to Ruth, and Ruth whispered back,

'You go and talk to her, I'll see to the tea.'

'What's your name?' the old lady asked.

'Caroline,' said Carly. 'But most people call me Carly.'

'I'm Amy Corby.' She was wearing a navy-blue coat, beautifully cut. Her shoes, gloves and handbag were expensive, and her silver hair was tucked under a navy velour hat. She was probably quite well off, although she could be in reduced circumstances and taking care of her clothes, but Carly felt sorry for her. Not just because she was old and had felt ill just now, but because she looked so lonely.

Suddenly Carly was convinced that she needed somebody to fuss over her, notice her, talk to her. She could imagine the kind of home she came from. Somewhere that had seen better days, although there would still be good pieces of furniture in it. Perhaps an apartment, or a bedsitter, where Amy Corby lived with her memories.

Carly was usually a fair judge of character. Usually she could sum up people pretty well, and the living-with-memories bit seemed confirmed when the old lady said, 'It was seeing that blouse in the window. Do you know, it's exactly like one I had in my trousseau over sixty years ago.'

She must be talking about the white blouse. It was pretty, square-necked with tiny tucks down the bodice, a classically simple style, but the fine lace-edged cuffs gave it a romantic air. They were floating, four-cornered, not practical but super for a dinner date so long as you managed to keep them out of the soup.

'We used to call them handkerchief sleeves,' Mrs Corby reminisced with shining eyes, and Carly smiled.

'But that's what they are—two Victorian handkerchiefs. And I thought I'd invented the idea of turning them into cuffs!'

'Did you make it?'

'Yes, I did—would you like to see it?'

Carly unhitched the blouse from the bamboo screen backing the window display and brought it across, and Mrs Corby gave a little cry of delight. 'Oh, it's exquisite! Beautifully made. Unfortunately it needs a young woman to wear it.' Her voice was wistful. 'But for a moment when I saw it I saw myself again when my throat and my hands were as smooth as yours.'

'I bet you were a smasher,' said Carly, and was rewarded with a gurgle of laughter.

'In my day that meant something rather different, but I was considered passably attractive.'

Carly could imagine her, fine-boned and fragile, cherished and protected. There weren't many like that in the world today. Carly herself was a girl of the times, tall, slim and strong, with wide-spaced slightly tilted eyes, full soft sensuous mouth and a firm clean jawline. Her hair, caramel-coloured, swung smooth and heavy as she turned to help Ruth, who was bringing in a tray and three tea-filled red enamel mugs.

Warmed by tea and company, Mrs Corby seemed in no hurry to leave. A few customers drifted in. A few bought, others were 'just looking'.

The boutique was making a living but a long way from making a fortune, and unless something fairly miraculous happened soon it would no longer be making anything, not for Ruth nor Carly. The lease was due for renewal and the asking figure could put them out of business.

That would be bad for Carly. She liked working here and living in a house just round the corner where she made her dresses, blouses, skirts, the way she enjoyed making them, with great care.

She was a practical girl, but the garments she fashioned were sheer romance. She designed around old lace, old fabrics, even old buttons or trimmings, and made each piece an individual. Some were elegant, some deliciously pretty, and they sold well. But there was a limit to the number she could turn out, prices had to be kept down to be competitive, and a lot of boutiques were going to the wall. Small shops were having hard times, and Ruth's was no exception.

Closing could be bad for Carly but not catastrophic. She had only herself to support. With health and energy she was pretty sure she would make out, but Ruth was different. Ruth was delicate, kind and sweet with brown velvet eyes, worrying over things that Carly shrugged at and coped with. But with a real worry looming now because if she lost her shop there wasn't much else she could do. Especially with William to consider.

William had just started school. He had been three years old when his father, Ruth's Jim, was killed on a motorbike; and Ruth had still been in a state of shock when she had first met Carly, sorting through some pieces of crochet in Stratford-on-Avon Oxfam.

The girls chatted. At that time Carly was working on a small collection of clothes that she planned to take around the local boutiques hoping for orders, and when Ruth expressed interest, explaining that she had a shop, Carly promised to be round in the morning with a caseful.

By next morning she had used some of the crochetwork as inserts in a linen wrapover skirt, and Ruth had been impressed.

The first customer had come in while they were putting one of the dresses in the window and Carly had found herself handling the sale. Ruth was a good salesgirl, considerate and anxious to help, but in those days her sadness was unbounded. She had to keep the business going and her small son clothed, washed and fed, when all she really wanted to do was lock herself away and grieve. Her eyes had filled with tears when she had told Carly she was a widow, and it was obvious that the bereavement was recent.

Carly stayed in the shop all day. At that time she was working in the evenings as a waitress in one of the town's hotels, a temporary job, and when Ruth said, 'I suppose you wouldn't consider coming here, would you? I need somebody around, I really do,' Carly agreed.

Afterwards Ruth insisted that bumping into Carly like that, in Oxfam, and turning to say, 'Sorry', had been the saving of her, because she had been drifting on a dark cloud for the previous two months. Relations and friends hadn't been able to give her lasting support, but Carly could handle the customers, and lighten the atmosphere of the little boutique which could easily have gone into a decline with Ruth.

William loved her. He had been a bewildered child in those days, not understanding what had changed his mother's smiling face out of recognition and taken his father away. But Carly came with arms that could lift him high, cuddling him and coaxing smiles from him.

It had been a good friendship. The girls had worked together compatibly for just over two years. For nearly as long as that Carly had shared Ruth's small terraced house, and William had grown into a merry small boy off to a real school, not play-school any more, and feeling very grown-up.

Ruth still missed Jim, but she had started going out on the occasional date, and if it hadn't been for the problem of the lease the future should have been promising.

Ruth might remarry, Carly thought. She would make any man a good wife, and Carly expected her to settle into marriage again some day.

'Never mind about me getting married,' Ruth would say. 'What about you? What's wrong with this one?'

'Not a lot,' Carly often had to admit, because some of the men who were attracted to her were all right—eligible, fanciable. Carly had no difficulty in filling her spare time. She had sex appeal, and something more. Ruth had sex appeal. Ruth was warm and womanly, but in Carly the attraction carried a challenge. There was a glint in her eyes, a style about her that made her stand out from the crowd.

But at nearly twenty-two she was still single and in no hurry at all to change her status . . .

Mrs Corby left, thanking them for the tea, and Carly watched her walking down the street, then turned to Ruth, who was just off to meet William out of school and take him home for his tea. Carly usually finished the afternoon in the shop on her own. 'I hope she'll be all right,' Carly murmured, and Ruth said reassuringly,

'I'm sure she will. She was fine after she'd had a little rest.'

Carly hadn't meant that Mrs Corby was likely to feel dizzy again, she had walked off straight and spry, but where was she going? Carly was convinced she had a lonely room somewhere, a lonely life, and although that was the fate of millions she found herself sighing. Life wasn't fair. There was poor Mrs Corby, and poor Ruth worrying herself sick about the lease.

'See you later,' said Ruth.

'Much later,' said Carly. 'Barney's picking me up from here.'

Barney was in insurance. He ran a Jaguar and enjoyed going around with Carly because she had the same dash and elegance. He lived in some style, to the very limits of his income, and was seriously considering asking her to move in with him.

Carly found him good company. His flat was very modern with a great deal of chrome and black glass, so that sometimes Carly felt she was moving through the showroom of a trendy furniture store. She knew that Barney had had other girl-friends staying there, but he was living alone now and she could read his mind that she looked well with the décor.

He arrived on the dot of six. He always did arrive on the dot, he was a predictable young man. She had had from half-past five to tidy the shop, lock up the till, freshen her make-up and change into a matching silk shirt and skirt, crushed raspberry colour. 'Very sexy,' said Barney, and Carly grinned, 'Why, it's just a little thing I ran up out of an old nightie.'

They were eating out tonight, the current in-place where they would meet clients and friends. The wine-lodge had been a boathouse until a few months ago and under the black beams lamps hung low, and outside the river glowed rose pink in the sunset, then cool grey and finally night-dark as the stars came out.

'Why do you keep staring out there?' Barney asked her. He had a nice smile, he was quite good-looking, and most of the time Carly had been looking at him, talking to him and friends. Now she shrugged.

'I don't know. Thinking of sailing away maybe, paddling off down the river.'

'Don't do that.' He put a hand over her hand on the table and pressed it gently, and she looked at his well-manicured fingers and thought how smooth his hands were. 'Why don't you move into my place?' he said softly. 'I get lonely for you.'

He almost whispered it, his lips so close to her ear that his breath fanned her cheek, and she said,

'I'll need to think about that.'

Barney wasn't flattered. He had hoped she would take up the offer, because it was a poky little house she lived in. They got on well together, he and Carly, so what did she need to think about? He said, 'All right, I suppose.' She knew he was considering whether he should give her a time limit, and told him the truth.

'It wouldn't be fair on you if I moved in, because I don't get lonely for anybody.'

Carly had never woken in the night and wished she could stretch out and touch him, or for that matter sat down on the sofa in front of the television and thought how much cosier it would be if Barney were there. And now she had hurt his pride and tried to make amends with a smile. 'I think yours is a lovely apartment and thanks for offering me a share of it, but I like to pay my own rent.'

'And you don't get lonely for anybody?' He picked up his brandy glass and looked at her over it. 'Aren't you the liberated lady?'

'Just lucky,' said Carly.

But when he kissed her goodnight in the car, outside Ruth's, he said, 'Think about what I said, about moving in with me.'

'Goodnight.' She slipped out of his arms and the car. 'And thanks again.' She would go out with him again, because she liked him, but she would never go home with him, to stay the night and the nights after.

She had turned her key and was opening the front door when he called through his wound-down window. 'You're a witch.' It was said admiringly, it was a compliment because she did bewitch him, and she laughed and walked into the hall and Ruth asked, with a spurt of laughter, '*What* did he just call you?'

Ruth was wearing a nightdress and carrying a mug

of hot milk. It was later than her usual bedtime, so she
probably hadn't been able to sleep, worrying about the
lease, probably. 'A *witch*,' said Carly. 'At least I think
that's what it was.'

'That's all right, then,' said Ruth. 'Have a good time?'

'I ate too much.'

'You'll burn it off,' said Ruth, wistfully because she
was plump and put on weight easily while Carly stayed
slim. 'He's nice, isn't he?'

'Oh, he is. He's just asked me to move in with him.'

Ruth waited, holding her mug of hot milk with both
hands. 'You really like him then?'

'Not enough to want him facing me over the breakfast table every morning.'

Ruth giggled. She was glad Carly wasn't going, the
relief made her giggle, 'You don't eat breakfast.'

A cup of black coffee and a piece of toast while Carly
dashed around was all there ever seemed time for, and
she grimaced, 'No, but I'll bet he does. Eggs and bacon
and probably fried bread. Besides, I'm still looking for
that millionaire.'

· That was one of their jokes, that Carly should find a
millionaire to back the business and buy the lease.
Sometimes Ruth half believed it might happen—not a
millionaire exactly, but Carly discovering some way
out. Ruth couldn't imagine Carly defeated, whereas
fear of failure had always been part of her own make-
up. She smiled, shaking her head, 'Well, please hurry
up about it. Do you want a drink?'

'Just bed,' said Carly, and yawned, then followed
Ruth upstairs to her own small room.

She wasn't tired. She would sleep, but not if she
started thinking about Ruth and William and their
future. Or her own future. After midnight was no time

to activate the mind. She got into bed and lay thinking drowsy thoughts, like Barney's offer tonight, which needed no consideration because it was a non-starter. She could never live with Barney, she would never want him so constantly close, but of course it wasn't true that she was never lonely. Everybody was lonely. She looked at the patch of starry sky between the pale drifting curtains and thought of Mrs Corby, and wondered if she slept peacefully and dreamed of happier days, and wished she had asked for her address. Tomorrow she would check local phone numbers and if she could track Mrs Corby she would invite her round here one evening, or perhaps to Sunday tea . . .

Ruth said why not, when Carly mentioned her plan next morning. 'You really took to that old lady, didn't you?'

'Yes, I did.' The shop was empty, Carly was sitting at the big desk in the little office sketching waistcoats and shirts that could incorporate some attractive braid motifs. 'Maybe I always wanted a grandmother.'

Ruth could remember her own grandparents and mother, although only her father was living now, but Carly was orphanage reared with no family at all. It hadn't seemed to bother her. She made friends easily, and Ruth and William were as close as a family. She had never shown any urge to 'adopt' a grandmother before, but something about Mrs Corby—spirit? courage?—had struck a chord of sympathy in her, and she really wanted to see the old lady again.

As it turned out she didn't need to do any detective work, because Mrs Corby came back. They had just opened after lunch when she strolled into the shop, and Carly greeted her with a wide smile, 'He*llo*!'

'I haven't come for more tea,' her smile was mischievous, 'but I lost a glove yesterday and I wondered if perhaps——'

Carly remembered the navy kid gloves she had been wearing. Today she was in silk gloves, the kid ones had probably been her best, and mislaying one could be a real loss. But it wasn't here, and Carly was almost sure that was just an excuse. Mrs Corby had popped in again because she had enjoyed sitting chatting.

Goodness knows, she did no harm. She was lonely, that was the trouble, and here was young vibrant life, young women earning a living, customers coming and going. She sat in the bamboo armchair and watched everything, as though it was part of a delightful play, and she was such a sweet old lady, and so clearly a woman of breeding and taste, that her nod of approval swayed more than one customer.

Carly chuckled as the door closed on a girl who had bought a party dress, 'You clinched that sale for us. She might have gone out without that if you hadn't said it was very pretty.'

'But it was,' said Mrs Corby.

'Well, I'm certainly glad you like our stuff,' said Carly. 'If you'd shaken your head she'd never have taken it. Do you have any daughters or granddaughters?'

'No.' A shadow fell over Mrs Corby's face—come to that, it could be *Miss* Corby—and Carly resolved to ask no more questions. But she answered them and so did Ruth. Ruth showed her a snapshot of William and said he was going to marry Carly when he grew up, he was quite determined on that; and Mrs Corby looked at Carly's hand and said, 'I noticed yesterday that you don't wear a ring, but of course you do have a special young man?'

'Not special,' said Carly. Special was not the word for Barney, nor for any of her men friends.

'I find that very hard to believe.' Mrs Corby sounded surprised and Ruth, said, smiling,

'It's her own fault. She could take her pick.'

'I just wish I could!' Carly was joking, but it had an element of truth. She could have been special to most of the men who had dated her, but she was too hard to please, too wary. Getting involved with the wrong man could drop you into a little hell. That was a lesson she had learned that she never talked about to anyone, not even to Ruth.

She said, 'I wonder, would you like to come to tea with us on Sunday?' and Mrs Corby's face lit up with pleasure.

'How kind of you! I should have liked that immensely, but—well it's my birthday on Sunday and I'm having a little party. Perhaps, instead, I could invite you?' She looked from one girl to the other, but her gaze stayed with Carly, and Ruth said hesitantly,

'Sunday's William's day. I always like to keep Sundays for him.'

Mrs Corby's eyes were still fixed on Carly as though she hadn't heard Ruth's excuse, and Carly knew exactly how it would be. All Mrs Corby's friends would be elderly. They would sip sherry and reminisce about the old days, and Carly would be quite out of place, but Mrs Corby's glance held real appeal and Carly said warmly, 'I'd love to.' She could look in and say hello and leave quite soon, but it would have been hurtful to refuse.

'Happy birthday,' she said, and turned to a display of large three-cornered kerchiefs that could be used as headscarves or shoulder-covering shawls. She had

edged them with braid or lace or fringe, and she
unlooped a pale lilac one, with a fringe edging, and
said, 'Wear this at your party. It's a birthday present.'

'Thank you, my dear.' The old lady's eyes misted.
'That's very generous of you, but it can't be good for
the profits if you're constantly giving things away.'

'Oh, but I'm not,' said Carly. 'Only to very special
people on very special days. I promise you I'm a
toughie.'

Mrs Corby looked hard at her. She had put on a
mock scowl, to get a smile, but Mrs Corby looked at
her straight and unsmiling, with a piercing directness
that made Carly blink. Then she said, 'Yes, I believe
you are,' and oddly she sounded pleased . . .

'Goodness knows what you've let yourself in for,'
said Ruth later. 'But I shouldn't think it's going to be
your sort of scene. And you've got to get all the way to
Cheltenham—I'd thought she was local.'

Mrs Corby had written her address for them, the
number, the street, and 'Cheltenham', which was about
twenty miles away. The party started at seven o'clock,
so that was Sunday evening gone, although if Mrs
Corby had come to tea Carly would have been happy
for her to stay until bedtime.

'Can I have the van?' she asked.

The elderly Mini van was their business transport,
although Carly had some very nice cars arriving to take
her out in the evenings. Perhaps she should have asked
Mrs Corby if she could bring a friend, then at least her
transport would have been provided. But offhand she
couldn't think of any man she knew who would want
to go to Mrs Corby's birthday party. They would treat
it as a joke—like Ruth said, it wasn't Carly's scene.
But Carly had been invited, and nobody was going to

ridicule Mrs Corby if she could help it, so she would have to go alone.

She dressed carefully, choosing a demure number in sprigged muslin, with high neck and long sleeves. If the full skirt had been longer it too might have looked like something out of Mrs Corby's trousseau. She didn't always wear her own creations. She had a wardrobe varying from plain classic to fun fashion, but Ruth said, 'Grandma should like that,' and William looked up, from a picture he was crayoning of a many-legged beast with fire coming out of its mouth, to ask, 'Whose grandma?'

'Mine,' said Carly, after getting down on her knees and reaching for a yellow crayon and brightening the 'fire'.

'Where did you get her from?'

'She just walked in.' William's eyes widened as he looked towards the door. He was still at an age of wishes-coming-true and she could see him wishing for a grandmother and said, 'You can share her if you like. I expect she walked in looking for you as well.'

She was sure that Mrs Corby wouldn't mind William adopting her. That could be another birthday present for a lonely old lady, a home at which she was welcome any time, and William said when could he see her. 'I'll ask her tonight,' Carly promised, and she grinned at Ruth, 'Suppose there's an old fat millionaire at the party, will he do?'

'Of course,' said Ruth. 'Just so long as he can write his name on a lovely fat cheque.'

Carly had checked the road map so that she knew the direction in which she was heading, and she was frowning thoughtfully for some minutes before she reached the square. There was nothing run-down about this area. These were fine Georgian houses. Most of them had brass plates on doors and rows of bells, but if Mrs Corby had an apartment here she was still living in some elegance. The cars parked in the roadway all looked several cuts above Carly's van, and Carly drove slowly, checking house numbers, finding '46' and going on driving, to stop round the first corner and park by a long wall.

Then she sat, considering. The front door had been closing as she'd passed, but she had glimpsed a chandelier and the magnificent stucco work of the ceiling, and heard music and laughter. That was no quiet little birthday party for a lonely old lady, counting the pennies.

Of course it had been pure assumption onCarly's part that Mrs Corby was lonely, or poor. She had never said she was, and Carly was delighted to find her living in such a beautiful house. From the looks of it nobody need 'adopt' her, although she had seemed nice enough to take the idea in good part, and come to tea and let William believe they had a special relationship.

Ruth was going to smile about this, Carly's lonely old lady living in this style.

Carly got out of the van and walked back, reaching the house just behind another couple who had parked across the road. The woman's dark fur coat matched her smooth dark hair, the man was silver-haired, and wearing a camel coat, and Carly shivered in her muslin dress, although when the front door opened warmth seemed to flow out.

The hall was breathtaking. Everything—walls, pictures, carpets—looked rich and colourful. A Georgian gem, like the pictures in beautiful home magazines.

She realised that someone was waiting for her name, a middle-aged man in dark jacket and pinstriped trousers, and thought—the old family retainer; and bit her lip, holding back a smile. 'Carly Brown,' she said.

'Would you come this way?'

The couple ahead of her were being greeted by others in the hall, as though they all knew each other well, and Carly trotted along behind Jeeves, or whatever his name was, into the drawing room.

She saw Mrs Corby at once, although it was a big room and almost full. Mrs Corby was sitting on a gilt armchair, and as Carly stepped forward, still following the dark jacket and pin-striped trousers, Mrs Corby leaned forward, holding out a hand.

Her rings flashed and Carly thought, she never took off her gloves. If she had done I'd have realised she was loaded. Oh, my gosh, the shawl!

Mrs. Corby was wearing a dress of deep violet silk, with Carly's lilac shawl pinned with an amethyst brooch, and Carly was touched, because that really was a gracious gesture. If Carly had been abashed by all this grandeur it would have restored her self-confidence.

Actually she was not overawed. It was a long time since she had envied anyone anything. A long time ago she had wished she was one of the children with homes and parents, but the orphanage hadn't been so bad. It had taught her self-reliance, and she went forward, smiling, although she knew that almost everyone in the room was watching her.

'I'm so glad you could come.' Mrs Corby squeezed her hand and inclined a cheek, and Carly bent and kissed it. She tasted of rose petals and with her hair groomed into deep soft waves and her skin warm and glowing she was quite beautiful. 'This is Roland,' she said, 'he knows all about you.'

I'll bet he doesn't, thought Carly, and found herself looking into a pair of bright blue eyes and an open friendly face with a super tan, and beautiful teeth. Husky and stunningly good-looking, he was the kind of man you always hope to meet at a party. 'Now see that Carly enjoys herself,' said Mrs Corby.

His voice too, when he said, 'It'll be my pleasure,' was just deep enough to be sexy, and just amused enough to make you feel he would be good company. He took Carly's arm, as though he was used to propelling girls around, and suggested, 'Can I offer you food? There's rather a good buffet.'

He certainly could. She had eaten before she came out, but she was sure this buffet would be spectacular, and she went with him past the other guests who were still looking at her, and obvious'y wondering about her. 'They're not going anywhere,' said Roland. 'I'll introduce you on the way back,' and Carly laughed,

'Don't worry. Even when they hear my name they won't have the slightest idea who I am.'

The walls of the dining room were deep blue with a great shimmering chandelier, and a buffet glittering jewel-like on a long, long table. I do wish Ruth had come, Carly thought. This is so pretty. I wish I could take some of it home for William.

Roland produced two glasses of champagne and asked what she fancied, and she said, 'What I need is a few minutes to get my breath back. I thought I was coming to a gathering of a few old friends in a little bedsitter. I thought Mrs Corby was a poor old lady, living by herself.'

He chuckled, laughter wrinkles deepening beside his

eyes, 'Not quite, no. Also her name is Madame Corbé.'

'Oh dear.' The champagne bubbles tickled her nose. It was delicious, but she must remember she was driving the van back. 'I don't get much right, do I?'

'Oh yes, you do.' He was looking at her with complete approval, telling her, 'Aunt Aimée's been speaking very highly of you.'

'That's nice. Is she your aunt?'

'Not exactly. My grandfather was her cousin. I'm from the English branch, she *is* the French branch.' So that explained the accent Carly had thought she'd noticed.

He put down his glass and picked up a plate. 'Now,' he said, hovering above the assorted salads, 'how about this?'

As she settled herself on a small footstool, with her plate full of canapés, Roland standing beside her, the woman who had come into the house just ahead of her and was heading for the buffet, asked him, 'Where's Liam?'

'He'll be along,' said Roland, and explained to Carly, 'My brother.'

'There are *two* of you?' She made her voice gleeful, she knew that Roland was attracted to her and it was mutual, and she wouldn't be surprised if it developed. He looked horrified.

'Not at all. Liam's nothing like me. We're both bachelors, but that's the only thing we've got in common, and I'm much better looking.'

He was joking, although he was the most attractive man in the room so far as Carly could see. 'Of course you are,' she said. 'You're so lovely that two of you could be too much of a good thing.'

'So are you.' The raillery had almost left his voice, and she said,

'Well, thank you.'

'Aunt Aimée's been talking about you ever since you took her in and gave her that cup of tea.'

'It was a small enough thing to do.'

Roland sat down beside her stool, on the deep dark blue carpet, so that they were almost face to face. 'Tonight I'm very grateful to her,' he said, 'for asking you along.'

'I'm grateful too,' said Carly, selecting her next mouthful from her plate and speaking in muffled tones, 'because this is a delicious party.'

'My brother Liam,' said Roland, 'isn't as good-looking as me, and I have a much nicer nature, but usually—I can't think why—he gets the gorgeous birds. But tonight I've got the winner.'

She had no doubt at all that Roland had had any number of winners, but this nonsense he was talking was fun, and she couldn't remember ever enjoying an evening more. Roland—whose surname was Sherrard —never left her. He introduced her all round, and although she knew none of them and none of them knew her, her striking looks and easy manner made her instantly acceptable. Sometimes she was asked what she did for a living and she said, 'I make clothes, to my own designs,' which might even bring in a few customers, because several of the women were interested enough to enquire about the boutique.

Roland ran his aunt's estates. He told Carly that when they were out in the walled garden behind the house. 'Would you like to see the garden?' he suggested, and of course she said yes.

The house was so spacious that she expected wide

lawns, which was stupid because this was a terraced house, and they stepped out into this small walled paved garden, a profusion of flowers and shrubs, with rough stone steps leading to a higher level, and statues and large urns, and she exclaimed, 'It's perfect! Everything about this place is magical.'

There was no one else here, and she went just ahead of him up the steps to the statue standing on a plinth at the far end, head and shoulders of a bewhiskered gentleman. 'Is he family?' she asked. 'He couldn't be brother Liam, could he?'

She was fooling. Anyone could see that he was early Victorian, and Roland burst out laughing, 'Not even without the whiskers.'

'I'm glad about that. He looks bad-tempered.' In the moonlight the beetling brows seemed scowling.

'So's Liam,' said Roland cheerfully. 'I keep telling you, I'm the good-tempered, good-looking Sherrard.'

'So you do,' she said, 'and so you are, I'm sure.' She patted his arm, and knew he would kiss her if she stood still and silent for a moment. 'Is he anyone in particular?' she asked.

'Five generations back,' said Roland. *Five?* She couldn't go back one. 'Maitre Louis Mathieu, the terror of the footpads. The bright boys in our family have usually gone in for the law. Liam's a barrister.'

'And what are you?'

'You mean how do I make a living?' Carly could make a guess at what he was—a cheerful charmer, who seemed a very nice man. What did he do? she meant. 'I run Aunt Aimée's estates in Brittany,' he said. 'We're here on holiday, going back in a few days, which doesn't leave a lot of time, so what are you doing tomorrow night?'

It was a pity she would be losing him so soon, but tomorrow night sounded a good idea. 'Would you believe washing my hair?' she asked.

'It smells beautifully clean to me.' Roland put an arm around her and nuzzled the top of her head. 'So may I take you and your hair out to dinner?'

'Thank you,' she said, 'I'd like that.'

She didn't think Madame Corbé would mind, because she smiled when she saw Roland still enthusiastically escorting Carly. She had left her chair and was walking around the drawing room among her guests and she smiled across at them, Roland with an arm around Carly, when there was a flurry near the door leading into the hall.

A man and a girl came in and everybody turned towards them, and Carly heard them saying Liam's name, as though they had been waiting for him, although it was Madame Corbé's birthday and so far as Carly could see the party had lacked nothing up to now.

. The girl looked ravishing enough to be an actress, in a sea-green floating dress, her pale skin quite flawless, her eyes huge with long black lashes in a heart-shaped face. She had a piping little-girl voice, trilling hellos, and hurrying across to Madame Corbé. The girl was effusive, but Madame Corbé didn't offer her cheek to be kissed as she had when she'd greeted Carly, and Carly thought, there isn't much love lost there, perhaps she's too gushing.

She stood back as Roland joined his brother, asking about the delay, which Liam explained with a shrug, 'Business, you know how it is,' and decided that Roland might have been joking, but it was true that he was better looking than Liam. Liam was taller, as broad in the shoulders but thinner, with a dark hawkish face.

There was no resemblance at all, except that they were both smiling and both had excellent teeth. Liam was the clever one—'The bright boys in our family have usually gone in for the law,' Roland had said—and Carly thought, he looks as though he thinks he knows all the answers. She felt none of the instant rapport she had felt with Roland. On the contrary, there was something disturbing about Liam Sherrard, even when you were only standing on the sidelines looking at him, and Carly found herself edging farther away, suddenly wanting to merge into the crowd. Then she heard Roland call, 'Carly!' and went through the guests towards the little family group.

'You haven't met Carly, have you?' said Madame Corbé, and Carly met Liam Sherrard's eyes. She had expected the impersonal stare and token smile of a stranger, but as he looked straight at her the smile stiffened on her lips as though she had turned to stone. The end of a lovely evening, she thought, and the end of a lovely friendship. He knows. . . .

CHAPTER TWO

LIAM SHERRARD didn't move a muscle, just stood there looking at her, arms folded, and for an age that could only have been seconds she was literally unable to say a word or take a step. Then, with an immense effort, she made herself start walking again.

Incredibly nobody seemed to have noticed that

looking him full in the face had hit Carly like a blow.
Her mind was still whirling. He was a barrister, he
could easily have been around during the court case.
Somewhere in her subconscious a memory stirred of
that dark watchful face so that she half expected him
to say, 'Haven't we met before?' or even, 'How's it
gone with you, Miss Brown, since your boy-friend
went down for burglary?'

'This is Carly,' Roland was saying, looking pleased
as though he had found her himself, and Carly felt
sorry for him because he probably wouldn't feel proud
of her much longer. 'Carly, this is Victoria Hayden,
and that brother of mine I was telling you about.'

The girl called Victoria murmured hello, her huge
eyes evaluating Carly like a cash register: face, figure,
clothes. Liam said, 'How do you do,' and Carly had an
hysterical urge to answer,

'Honestly, believe it or not. The way I always have
done.'

Then she realised that Madame Corbé had a hand
on her arm and was looking at Liam as though
something exciting was happening.

'Well?' she was saying. 'Well?'

'Well what?' asked Liam.

'Who does she remind you of?'

Carly's face went blank. Liam and Roland exchanged
glances. Roland shrugged, bewildered; Liam said, 'I
have no idea.'

Yes, you have, thought Carly, and I can understand
how you know, but what is my little old lady talking
about?

Madame Corbé sounded disappointed. 'I did hope
Roland might have seen it, but I was sure you would,
Liam.'

'I give up,' said Liam. 'You tell us.'

'I shall show you.' She tightened her grip on Carly's arm. 'Come,' she said imperiously, and swept Carly out of the room with a word here and a smile there. Like a royal progress, Carly thought, with the two princes following behind, and the lady Victoria twittering in the rear.

Carly hadn't a clue what was going on. It would have been intriguing and amusing if Liam Sherrard hadn't arrived, but he had brought bitter memories and she felt slightly sick. Although the beauty of the graceful staircase, and the cool femininity of the bedroom into which Madame Corbé led her little procession, were soothing in their way.

There were bowls and vases of yellow roses all around, the room was like a bower, and Madame Corbé took Carly to the dressing table and picked up a photograph in a thin oval silver frame.

'Now,' she said to Liam and Roland, 'you see it, don't you?' She was almost pleading, as if she very much wanted them to agree with her and Victoria squeaked, 'Who *is* it?'

Nobody answered. No one else had followed upstairs, and Roland took the silver frame and looked at the coloured photograph and then at Carly and said, 'Yes, I think there is a likeness.' He held it for Carly to see, a young girl, with high cheekbones and honey-coloured hair cut in a fringe and bob, sitting on a rock, the sea behind her.

She thought there was a family resemblance to Madame Corbé rather than a likeness to herself. The child looked delicate, but Madame Corbé was explaining eagerly, 'The colouring, you see, the hair. That used to swing when she moved her head, the way

Carly's does. And her gestures. And she was a kind
girl. She would have brought an old lady in for a cup
of tea like you did.' Tears glittered in her eyes and
Carly put an arm around her shoulders.

'I'm sure she would,' she said.

'She was my granddaughter,' said Madame Corbé.
'You look like my granddaughter.'

That was a coincidence, considering that Carly had
talked about adopting her as a grandmother. The ima-
ginary resemblance seemed to be pleasing her, and
Carly asked gently, 'You lost her?'

'Nearly twenty years ago, just after this photograph
was taken. She was a beautiful girl. Wasn't she beautiful?'

She looked again at Liam and Roland, and Roland
said, 'Indeed she was.'

'She was,' Liam said crisply. 'But she looked like
you, Aunt Aimée, and not in the least like Miss
Brown.'

The light went out in Madame Corbé's face. She
had wanted to talk about her granddaughter, Carly
could see that she would have launched into
memories—not all of them sad, she had been starting
to smile—but when Liam spoke her lips closed tremu-
lously. Then she asked, 'How old are you, Carly?'

'Twenty-one,' said Carly. And eleven months.

'Antoinette would have been twenty-nine, she was
Roland's age, but I think she might have grown up
looking like you,' and Carly said,

'I'd like to hear about her, I really would.'

'Not tonight,' said Liam to Madame Corbé. 'Not
while you've getting on for fifty folk cluttering up the
drawing room. Your place is down there, my beauty,
you're the one they're here to see. You can talk with

Miss Brown another time.'

Madame Corbé was a hostess of the old school. Reminded of her duties to her guests, she responded automatically, 'But of course we must go down again.'

She took Liam's arm, which he offered with a smile, and as they went he began telling her some story that made her laugh. The silvery sound of her laughter drifted back as Carly picked up the photograph again and asked Roland, 'What was she like?'

'Aunt Aimée's pride and joy,' he said. 'She never goes anywhere without that photograph even now. It was taken that last summer. We always went over there for the school holidays, Liam and I, she was like a sister to us, a smashing kid. She caught pneumonia, a chill, and suddenly she'd gone.' He sighed, his cheerful face grave. 'I suppose it was nearly twenty years ago— Lord, how time flies!' and Carly knew that for a moment he had been reliving holidays of long ago.

For her school holidays hadn't differed much from term-time, except that there were no lessons. Most of the children had somewhere to go, somebody who wanted them for some of the time, but Carly usually stayed in the orphanage. She hadn't been unhappy, she had been busy, helping in the gardens and the buildings, but the fun of long lazy days, family holidays, had never been her lot.

How tragic that the little girl who had everything should have slipped away like that. She must have had a fabulous time when holidays came round and the two English boys who were like her brothers came: riding, swimming, running barefoot along beaches. Carly could imagine Roland, his face was still boyish, and Liam would have been a tall thin studious boy, and the girl walking between them had had hair the colour of her own.

'*Am* I like her?' she asked. Her reflection in the gilt-framed mirror over the dressing table didn't answer her question. There was the age difference, and Carly's face was stronger, lacking the soft prettiness of the child's.

'Probably,' said Roland after a moment's hesitation. 'I can't remember too clearly how she looked, I was only nine when she died. I can see her again when I look at photographs, of course, and probably Aunt Aimée's right and she might have grown up looking something like you.'

But not like me, she thought. Not like me inside at all. 'Pity we have to go down and join them,' said Roland, putting practised arms around her and kissing her with gentle ardour. And it was warm and pleasant and after the kiss they would certainly join the others, because there was no passion. This was just a moment of mutual appreciation, and when Carly turned her head they were reflected in the mirror looking very well together, her slim white figure entwined with his tall dark-suited body.

But she had no time to admire the picture they made, because Liam was also reflected in the dressing table mirror. He stood just inside the doorway, arms folded, viewing them with what seemed to be cynical detachment.

'Do you usually pussyfoot around like this?' she asked his reflection, and Roland turned and saw his brother and grinned as Liam said,

'All the time, in my own house.'

'Yours, is it?'

'Afraid so.' Liam opened a drawer in a white bow-fronted chest of drawers and took out a small flat bottle, explaining, 'Aunt Aimée's smelling salts. We're getting a little short on oxygen down there.' But Carly wondered if he had doubled back because he was unwilling to leave her in the bedrooms with Roland, and finding them kissing could have confirmed his suspicions. 'I hate to spoil anything more interesting,' he said, 'but I think you should be rejoining the party.'

'I hate to agree with you,' said Roland. He was still holding Carly, still smiling at her, asking Liam, 'But isn't she gorgeous? Wouldn't you find it hard to keep your hands off her?'

'Difficult,' said Liam drily, 'but fortunately not impossible,' and Carly found herself looking at his hands and thinking, I'd hate them on me, because she knew quite surely that the touch would be no caress.

'What's with "Miss Brown"?' asked Roland as the three of them came down the staircase. 'Why not Carly?'

'An unusual name. Is it short for anything?' Liam sounded casual, but he was watching her face as closely as if this was evidence in a courtroom, and she said,

'It's short for Caroline,' repeating, 'Caroline Brown.' She looked straight at him because she didn't like him, but she wasn't having him imagine that she was scared of him, and in turning to look up put her foot not quite squarely on the narrow shallow step. She would probably have regained her balance, but as she lurched slightly Liam grabbed her shoulder making her gasp. The grip was hard enough to bruise, although his voice sounded deceptively considerate. 'Do watch your step, Caroline.'

'Thank you,' she said, 'that was quick. Rather too quick, because I wasn't falling. And by the way, nobody calls me Caroline. If you can't manage Carly let's stay with Miss Brown.'

She said it laughing, and he laughed too, 'Oh, I'm sure I can manage Carly,' and she was pretty sure that was a threat and his laughter went no deeper than hers.

She didn't enjoy what was left of the party. Roland was just as attentive and just as charming, but even while she was smiling and flirting with him she was searching for Liam. No, not searching, she never looked around deliberately for him, but it was as though she had turned bionic so that she could sense his presence anywhere in the crowded rooms. Because every time she did glance up she seemed to meet his eyes.

She couldn't relax when her nerves were twanging, and the atmosphere was thickening with cigarette smoke and the hot air of a barrage of talk and perfume and after-shave and overheated bodies. She could understand why Madame Corbé had wanted her smelling salts, although Madame Corbé still looked cool and composed. It only seemed to be Carly who was finding it hard to breathe.

They danced, she and Roland. When another man asked her for a dance Roland said, 'Sorry, she's fully booked,' and that was flattering, but although the doors to the little walled garden were open now and the dancers were swaying around out there Carly still felt breathless even in the open air. Probably because as she went out with Roland Liam had said, 'It's rugged underfoot. Remember what I told you, watch your step.'

He had been standing with his back to Carly and Victoria hanging on to his arm. 'Your brother doesn't miss much, does he?' she said to Roland.

The music was soft out here, and there was only room for about half a dozen couples. Roland's arms were around her waist and she moved with him to the beat. 'No,' he agreed. 'But what made you say that?'

Because he was watching her like a hawk, she could feel his eyes like talons. Because he knew her—or thought he did. If she and Roland had been alone out here she would have walked to the end of the garden, where there was a little stone seat, and sat down and said, 'I think I've met Liam before.' Then she would have told him about Gerald.

She was sure that Liam would tell him when the party was over, and afterwards maybe Roland wouldn't turn up for their evening date. It could sound very unsavoury, because of course Liam's account would put Carly in the worst possible light.

But if Roland did come then Carly would tell her side of the story and he could please himself what he believed. She couldn't get in ahead tonight, this was not the time nor the place for intimate confessions, and if Roland let himself be brainwashed by Liam then she could do without Roland.

'Well?' queried Roland. 'What makes you think Liam doesn't miss anything?'

She danced on, almost on the spot, her heavy hair swishing. 'Well, he saw us coming out here although he had his back to us.'

'Heard us, more likely,' said Roland.

'And he looks sharp.'

'Granted. As a razor.'

'Sharp and prejudiced,' she said, and surprise made Roland loose his tenuous hold on her and fling out his hands in protest, demanding, 'What?'

'He doesn't like me.'

'Rubbish!' Roland's reaction was emphatic and sincere. He hadn't sensed the antagonism, and for a moment she wondered if she had been over-reacting. 'Of course he likes you,' said Roland. He cupped her shoulders. 'Not as much as I do, of course,' and she flinched slightly merging the movement into the dance. She was going to have five separate bruises on her right shoulder, Liam Sherrard's fingerprints, and she saw his tall figure silhouetted in the doorway as he and Victoria came out.

'Shall we ask him?' Roland suggested, smiling, following her gaze, and suddenly Carly was tired of the whole thing. It was late and she had to be up early. She said, 'I really should be going home,' and gently overriding Roland's protests headed for the door back into the house.

'Goodnight,' she said brightly to Liam and Victoria.

'Leaving so soon?' Liam enquired.

'I start work early.'

'You make clothes, I hear.' That was Victoria, sounding as though Carly was a little sewing woman stitching away in an attic.

This was the first patronising touch Carly had encountered tonight, Victoria wasn't gushing now, she was practically sneering, and Carly decided she was very suitable for Liam.

'That's right, yes,' Carly drawled. 'Do you make anything?' and Victoria went into the giggles.

'Oh yes,' she batted her lashes at Liam. 'And I'm good at it too, aren't I, darling?'

She obviously meant making love, and Carly said, 'I should watch him if I were you. He only helped me downstairs and I'm black and blue.'

She found Madame Corbé and said, 'It's a lovely

party, I've enjoyed myself enormously, only I have to get up in the morning.'

'Goodnight, my dear.' Madame Corbé raised her face again to be kissed, and Carly felt a strange pang, an urge to say something like—please don't listen to Liam, he doesn't know it all, I promise you. 'I shall see you again before we leave,' said Madame Corbé, squeezing Carly's hands, and Carly said, 'I do hope so.'

'I'm seeing Carly tomorrow night,' said Roland, though it was tonight, actually, and Madame Corbé looked pleased and Carly said, 'I wonder, please could I take a few cakes back for William?'

She was leaving with a large cardboard box of assorted party bites when Liam loomed up again in the entrance hall and she said, 'Cakes. Would you like to check? No silverware. Just cakes for a small boy.'

'Yours?'

'The boy? No. A friend's.'

She wasn't absolutely certain, of course, that he had recognised her, although there was the niggling feeling at the back of her own mind that she had seen him some time during her blackest hours. But even if she had it was possible that he couldn't quite place her yet. Nearly four years had passed, perhaps it was nagging him too, the face, the name. She might still have time to get in her story first, and she went out of the house with Roland.

He had asked how she was getting home and she had explained, 'I've brought a car.' She had parked just round the corner, and they walked with his arm around her in silence. When they reached the van and she dug into her purse for the key he said, 'Is this it?'

'It's hardly one I'd be stealing, is it?' It was an ancient model, and he laughed, and Carly wished she hadn't said 'stealing'. Now she could say, 'Come in and sit down—I've got something to tell you before Liam does.' But she was tired, and the prospect of spelling out that old miserable story was daunting. She couldn't do it. The words would stick. Tomorrow she would—if he came tomorrow.

'Goodnight, then,' said Roland, and kissed her lightly on the lips, tilting her chin to raise her face to his. 'Half past seven, and I'll count the hours.'

She was sure he said that quite often, and she nodded, 'Seven-thirty, you know where to find me . . .'

The bedside light was still on in Ruth's room and her door was ajar. She was reading, pillows propped up behind her, and as Carly passed she called, 'Have fun?'

'You're keeping late nights.' Carly came into the room. Ruth had always been slightly insomniac, but lately it had been worse.

'Look who's talking,' said Ruth. But when Carly wasn't out on a date she slept a sound seven and a half hours, and now she sat on the side of the bed and said,

'Was I wrong about our little old lady! She has estates in Brittany—she's French, and you should have seen the house the party was held in!' As she described it, and the guests, Ruth's eyes grew wider. 'What with Daimlers and Rolls and Jags,' said Carly, 'I was so sorry for our old van that I parked her round the corner.' She grinned. 'Well, you know how sensitive she is, it could have given her a complex. Honestly, I was bowled over, everything was fabulous! And rich. If Madame Corbé had taken her gloves off in the shop and we'd seen her rings we'd have known she could buy and sell us.'

'I suppose she wouldn't like to buy us?' said Ruth wistfully.

Carly hadn't thought about that, but Madame Corbé had admired her work, and she did seem to be interested in the boutique, and perhaps she might consider a business proposal.

'Or maybe you found your millionaire?' Ruth was joking now, and Carly laughed,

'You wait and see who's calling for me after work tonight! His name's Roland Sherrard and he's related to Madame Corbé. He runs the estates and he's gorgeous.'

She closed her eyes, hugging herself with an exaggeratedly blissful expression, and Ruth squealed, 'It isn't true! You're pulling my leg.'

'It is so true.' Carly had put down the box by the bed and she bent now to lift it up. 'And here's William's take-home party to prove it. I thought I'd leave it in my room and he could have it when he got in from school. Down in the kitchen he might have fancied it for breakfast.'

The member of staff who had been told to pack some buffet remains for a small boy had arranged cakes and savouries attractively. It could have been a window centrepiece, and Ruth gasped, and in the connecting doorway that led to his bedroom William asked, 'Is it for me? Can I see it?'

He was yawning and bleary-eyed, but he had heard the bit about 'William's take-home party,' so he was allowed one sausage roll and then tucked firmly back into bed. Ruth switched off her light as Carly went and Carly went out like a light the moment her head touched the pillow.

She woke a few minutes before she had to get up, and lay there reliving the party. There was plenty more to tell Ruth: that Madame Corbé thought she looked like Antoinette, that Roland had a brother.

Where had Carly seen Liam Sherrard? He was familiar, in a nightmarish way. She felt she should know him, but she couldn't put a background to him. It was only the face she remembered, and she concentrated on that so fiercely that her head started to ache.

She got up and went to the bathroom and washed her face in cold water and thought, I don't need to be scared of him, he can't do anything that can really hurt me. If he puts Roland off me it won't break my heart, because my heart isn't involved with Roland. I just like him, and anyway, he's away before the end of the week.

This morning she was confident that Roland would come tonight, and she would put Liam right out of her mind. The bruises on her shoulder were lighter than she'd expected, they would soon fade, so there was no reason for this pounding surge of panic that rose up in her every time she 'saw' Liam Sherrard's face.

She didn't mention him to Ruth. During their usual rush at breakfast time Ruth asked, gulping her coffee, 'Was it really like you said last night?'

'Just like I said,' said Carly.

'Wow!' said Ruth. 'Well, I can't wait to meet the millionaire.'

The day was busy, there wasn't much chance for chatting, and when Ruth left Carly, to collect William from school, they had had no further discussion about last night. Carly was looking forward to seeing Roland again. She was also prepared to tell him about Gerald, although she wasn't looking forward to it. It was a long time since she had had to dwell on it, and it was of course no business whatever of Roland's, except to set the record straight if brother Liam had come out with a biased version.

The shop was empty a few minutes before closing time, and Carly was wondering whether to shut and go home and wash her hair in the extra ten minutes, when the phone rang. It was Ruth, and her voice sounded odd, a sort of hissing whisper, 'He's *here*!'

'Who is?'

'Your date.' Half past seven, he'd said, and it wasn't yet half past five. This was more than over-eager, it was very inconvenient. Or perhaps he'd come to explain why he couldn't manage their dinner after all. 'Give him a cup of tea,' said Carly, 'and I'll be right with you.'

Ruth giggled, and that sounded nervous too, 'You'd better hurry, because William's just asked him if he's the milanare you met last night.'

'The what?'

'Millionaire. He must have heard us talking.'

'Well, it was only a joke,' said Carly, and Ruth said, 'I know that, but it didn't make him laugh. I tried to explain, but he didn't seem amused.' Her voice quickened until she was gabbling, 'He's been asking me about you. And I've been telling him how popular you are and how well you get on with folk, the customers and everybody, and how you like Madame Corbé. But he doesn't look happy about it.'

There was a tightness in Carly's throat so that she had to swallow before she could say, 'I think you might have the wrong one.'

'What do you mean? He said his name was Sherrard.'

'Dark hair? A lot? Tall and thin and hatchet-faced?'

'Very good-looking, though, very aristocratic.'

Carly swallowed again. 'That's Liam, Roland's brother. Keep William away from him, and don't you say anything about anything except the weather.'

'Hurry *up*,' begged Ruth. 'He's got me so nervous I can't stop babbling!'

'That's Liam,' said Carly. 'He's a lawyer. I bet he's lethal at grilling the suspects.' She put down the phone as she spoke and rushed around, switching off, then grabbed her coat and was dashing out of the door as a woman almost bumped into her.

'Are you shutting?' snapped the woman, sounding aggrieved, and Carly said,

'Yes—sorry. Please come back tomorrow,' and raced down off the road so fast that the woman wasted no time in moving away herself. You never knew these days, there could have been a bomb in there.

The Mercedes outside the house had to be Liam Sherrard's and Carly resisted an impulse to kick the tires. How dared he come here and bother Ruth? How dared he come here at all? The house door was on the latch and she hurried along the little hall to the living room where Ruth was sitting on the settee, an arm protectively around William, and Liam Sherrard stood up as Carly swept in.

He was wearing a beautifully tailored grey suit, grey silk shirt and tie. A man that tall and thin would look elegant in anything, but his suit must have cost a fortune. Thin-lipped and hooded-eyed, he surveyed her with distaste, this was not going to be a friendly meeting, and she said shrilly, 'I don't remember asking you around.'

She was wishing now that she had walked from the

shop instead of running, then she might not have been breathless and her hair wouldn't be flopping into her eyes. She tossed back her hair and he said, 'I apologise—obviously I should have phoned for an appointment,' making her sound a conceited idiot.

'What do you want?' The angry colour was burning in her cheeks, and Ruth and William were staring, they had never seen Carly like this, and Ruth got up, stammering, 'I—er——'

'Don't you go,' said Carly, and to Liam, with edgy politeness, 'Perhaps you'd like to come into the workroom.'

Her sewing room was the front room. The only furniture was a large table and one chair, a big old-fashioned chest of drawers and a full-length mirror. Her sewing machine was on the table, and a half completed dress. Other garments hung on hangers from a wall rail.

'Right,' said Carly, almost before he was in the room, 'now what?'

She shouldn't be carrying on like this. She didn't need an enemy. Whatever he had come to say she should have stayed calm, but somehow Liam Sherrard managed to get under her skin and trigger a gut reaction, although she didn't know whether it was fear or fury churning inside her. As he closed the door behind him she said, 'We have met before, of course.'

'No.' He was looking around as though the room interested him more than she did, and while she was blinking with surprise at his denial he added, 'A friend of mine defended Gerald Collett.'

'Nice friends,' she drawled. She could remember that friend. He had been large and florid-faced, looking like everybody's favourite uncle, and had pleaded

Gerald's case so fervently that Carly had half expected a verdict of Not Guilty. That would have been something of a record, as Gerald had admitted breaking into half a dozen houses that winter and stealing money and goods.

It had been terrible, seeing Gerald in the dock, with all the promise of his future in ruins. He had had promise or he wouldn't have been up at university. He and Carly had met at a rag-week dance, and the attraction had been instant and mutual. She was working as a salesgirl in one of the multiple stores, but a lot of her friends were students—she was as bright as most of them, brighter than many—and she fell in love with Gerald.

She wouldn't have cared if he had had no more than his grant, it had just seemed a lovely bonus that he had money. He spent freely, and assured her that was what money was for, bought her presents, and said she was the most exciting girl he had ever come across. He asked her to marry him. Not yet, when he finished with college, and brought her a ring—a sparkling diamond cluster—and she was packing, because a crowd of them were going to Spain for Christmas, when the knock came on the door.

It would have been her first holiday abroad, and ever since the plan got under way she had hardly slept nights for excitement. She thought it was Gerald, come a little early to collect her and her case. But it was the police, a man and a woman, and that was when the nightmare began.

Carly changed during the next half hour, growing older, more worldly. She had been completely unprepared for the news that the money Gerald had spent so freely—and not only on her, he had expensive tastes all round—belonged to somebody else. Like the ring on her finger. He was a thief, and caught, he had admitted it, and Carly, he had said, was the reason.

He denied that she knew the gifts she had received were stolen goods, but when she was called in evidence in the Crown Court his counsel made it clear that in his opinion she should have been standing in the dock beside Gerald. She was the gold-digger, the grabber, the girl who had infatuated an impressionable young man. He had turned to crime to give her a good time, because he had known that if he didn't she would soon find someone else who would.

Carly had felt guilty enough about the money she had helped him spend. She blamed herself, although she had never for a moment suspected how he was acquiring it. She had wanted to repay, and would have been prepared to hand over wages, but nobody seemed to take that seriously for a minute, and although Gerald was the guilty one the mud was flung at her until she felt she could never be clean of it. That was when she had seen Liam Sherrard. She had looked up into the public gallery while Liam Sherrard's friend, Gerald's counsel, was hammering away at her and seen him. There had been others come to watch, people she knew, but she remembered his dark face, sitting up there in judgment on her.

'I was in court,' he said. 'I'd been on another case and I was staying with the Morrisons.' Gerald's barrister was Morrison. 'I presume you weren't waiting for Gerald Collett when he came out of prison?'

'No,' she said.

Gerald had been jailed for twelve months, and outside the court his father had told her to keep away. He was a thin balding man, Gerald's father, his mother was small and might have been pretty, and they both looked at Carly as though they wished she would drop dead—and who could blame them when they believed she had ruined their son? His father handed over a letter from Gerald, and although she tore it up, as soon as she was alone, she would always remember every word of it. It was bitter and cruel, hitting out at her, blaming her, and she had never completely trusted a man since.

'I'd have expected you to have done rather better than this for yourself,' said Liam Sherrard. The workroom didn't look very impressive; come to that, neither did the house. 'Would you?' she said shortly. 'Well, I'm satisfied, thank you.'

'You surprise me.' His voice was a little like Roland's, but Liam drawled his words. 'I'd have put you down as one who was never satisfied.'

She was glaring, so of course she didn't look content and serene, and she demanded, 'Do you know Gerald?'

'No.'

'Then why have you got it in for me? What I said was true. I had no idea where the money was coming from.'

'You don't need to protest your innocence. You weren't on trial.' The words sounded reassuring, but the tone of the voice and the slight twist of the lips were cynical, and she thought, Oh yes, I was on trial. You judged me, for one. That's why you're here. 'My aunt's taken a fancy to you,' Liam continued, and Madame Corbé was not his aunt, but this was not the time to argue small details, and Carly said quietly,

'I've taken a fancy to her, I like her very much, she's a charming lady. There's something about her.' She hesitated. Madame Corbé had a host of attractive qualities, and Liam Sherrard suggested,

'Money?'

Her hand lifted of its own volition, outstretched to strike, and he said, 'If you do I shall have no hesitation at all in knocking you down.'

Carly locked her fingers together, gripping them because she couldn't trust that right hand, and sneered, 'You must be a lousy barrister if that's all the self-control you've got!'

'It wouldn't be lack of control hitting you back,' he informed her. 'It would be entirely premeditated.'

She believed him, and she believed he would do it. 'Isn't that nice?' she muttered through gritted teeth. 'Well, go on, there must be more. Have you come along to tell me Roland's remembered a previous engagement? I'm sure you told him all about Gerald.'

'No.' He shrugged. 'If I did I'm sure that your version would be more convincing. No, it's Aunt Aimée I'm concerned with. She's got this idea that you look like Antoinette.'

'Do I?' she asked impulsively, and wished she hadn't asked.

'Your hair's the same colour.' He looked at her and she felt naked, worse than naked, as though he could get inside her and read her mind, and she stiffened, trying to keep him out. 'Under the skin there is no similarity,' he said, 'but she wants to take you back with her on Friday, or failing that she wants you to follow as soon as you can.'

'You mean for a holiday?' That was very sweet of Madame Corbé, and a complete surprise. It would be lovely, but apart from her responsibilities here—she couldn't leave Ruth right now—she was not

Antoinette, and the slight resemblance would only cause pain, because the dead grandchild could never be replaced. She was about to say, 'That's kind, but I couldn't,' when Liam demanded, 'How much do you want to tell Roland tonight that you can't go?'

He really believed she was for sale. He thought she was opportunist all through, always with an eye to the main chance, and the blood roared in her ears and she smiled a slow and feline smile. 'Scared she might decide to adopt me, are you? Suppose I change my name to Antoinette, do you think that might help?'

'You're not Antoinette,' he said, and now his voice was clipped, 'and if you do go out there I'll see to it that you don't make a penny piece out of Madame Corbé. But if you turn down the invitation I'll meet any reasonable offer.'

'Ah, but what's reasonable?' Now Carly put on an expression like a cat with the cream. 'Do you think she might be changing her will?' She hardly knew what she was saying, she was so furious. 'Cutting you out and naming me?'

That was ridiculous, but flinging taunting words at him was the next best thing to hitting him, and he was turning white as though he was nearly as angry as she was. 'If I thought that pretending you were Antoinette would make her happy I'd wish you luck,' he said harshly, 'but I don't. I think you could cause her a lot of grief, and if that happened I promise you I'd see it came home to roost.'

They had been standing near each other, he by the door, she with her back to the table. She moved away to the window now. 'And Roland's going to pass on the invitation tonight, is he?' she said slowly. 'Then you'll have to wait, because I'll give him my answer. If it's no you can phone me and we'll discuss my terms, but if it's yes please, then that means I'm playing for higher stakes, and for all your bluster, Mr Sherrard, I don't think there'll be a blind thing you can do about it!'

Their gazes locked. Again Carly felt the shock wave, jerking her head back a fraction. Then Liam turned and went, leaving this door open, closing the front door behind him. She watched him get into his car. She could see his hands on the wheel as he sat for a moment or two motionless, and she knew he was steadying himself before he drove off.

He half turned his head, looking back at the window and she jumped away, but when she heard the car start up she craned forward again and watched it go down the road. Oh God, she hated him! His attitude was so brutally unfair. Of course, he was the face in the public gallery. She had looked up there while Gerald's counsel was cataloguing the gifts Gerald had given her. 'Yes,' she was saying, 'yes,' to each of them. And the diamond cluster ring . . . yes. She had looked up and in the sea of faces she had seen Liam Sherrard, handsome and arrogant and cruel, and thought, he could be a Ceasar up there, about to give the thumbs-down that would mean a knife in my heart.

The knives were out for her that day. The sympathy was for Gerald. He was the one facing the prison sentence. She had enjoyed the spoils and taken none of the risks. That was what Liam Sherrard had believed and still believed, and now he was convinced she was wondering what she could get out of Madame Corbé.

She couldn't go to Brittany. She would tell Roland tonight, but when Liam phoned to discuss the 'pay-off' she would tell him, 'You don't have anything I want,' and let him wonder if she was still going to turn up.

'Carly?' said Ruth, sounding as though she had spoken before and Carly hadn't heard. 'All right?'

'Oh yes,' said Carly.

'He's gone, then?'

'Uh-huh.' Ruth waited, and Carly told her, 'Tonight Roland's bringing an invitation from Madame Corbé for me to go out there for a holiday. To Brittany. Liam doesn't think it's a good idea.'

'Why ever not?' Ruth knew about Gerald, but it had happened before she met Carly and she had no doubts that Carly had been misled. They never talked about it, and while Carly was steeling herself to start explaining why Liam disliked her Ruth said, 'Well, I think it's a terrific idea. You could do with a holiday, and I could get one of the mothers to give me a hand in the shop for a few weeks. Don't you want to go?'

Just for a week, perhaps? A few days with Roland and Madame Corbé, not pretending to be Antoinette, being herself. It would be rather splendid, holidaying in a château, and it would show Liam Sherrard that he could neither bribe nor frighten her. He had looked down at her in that courtroom as though she was beneath contempt. For that she would like to disturb his well-ordered life.

He lived in England, worked here too, presumably, so he might not be able to get over to Brittany. He wouldn't know what Carly was up to, which would give him plenty to worry about, and she heard herself telling Ruth, 'Yes, I think I would like to go. If you could manage here I think I might enjoy myself very much.'

CHAPTER THREE

ROLAND was so different from Liam. For one thing, he was pleased to see her. When Carly opened the front door he beamed appreciatively and told her, 'You look absolutely stunning.'

She was quite pleased with her appearance. She had spent the last hour and a half slowly and soothingly glamorising herself, because that scene with Liam had left her feeling as though she had been dragged through a hedge backwards. She had gone to her bedroom and paced around like an angry cat, then caught a glimpse of herself in the mirror, glinting eyes and dishevelled hair, and remembered Roland and thought, I'll frighten him off if he sees me like this. It won't need brother Liam to warn him against me.

She had laughed at herself, but wryly, because it hadn't really been amusing, and set about preparing for her date. A bath and a hair wash, a blow-dry, and make-up put on with light fingertips, all helped to relax her. She was looking glowing and good when she came downstairs and joined Ruth and William, to wait for the doorbell to ring and Roland to collect her.

'So do you look stunning,' she told him now. 'Come in for half a minute while I get my handbag.' She knew that Ruth was dying to see him.

His car was a Porsche with a left-hand drive. It seemed odd having the passenger seat on the wrong side, but everything else was familiarly comfortable. He was quite like other friends she had, good-looking and good company, and they chattered and joked as though they had known each other for years.

She didn't mention that Liam had called on her until Roland brought up the holiday invitation, and that was just after Carly had made her selection from the sweet trolley. He had talked a lot about the Château des Sables, his home, the manor house of Madame Corbé's estate, which had stood since the seventeenth century overlooking the coastline of Brittany. 'It sounds beautiful,' she said, as she had several times before, and he said,

'You should see it. Why don't you come back with us for a holiday?' Carly had a fork poised over a strawberry gâteau. She cut off a small portion of sponge and he went on, 'It was my aunt's suggestion, but I think it would be a splendid idea.'

'Liam doesn't,' she said, and he gasped,

'How do you know?'

Liam must have made his disapproval clear, but if he hadn't mentioned Gerald what reason had he given? She said, 'He called on me tonight. He was waiting at the house when I got back from work,' and this time Roland's gasp was even louder.

'*Did* he? I hadn't realised he felt that strongly. I suppose it's because Aunt Aimée's got this bee in her bonnet about Antoinette. He doesn't want her reminded. She's old and she isn't very strong.'

'It isn't just that,' said Carly slowly. 'He thinks I might take advantage of the situation, looking like her granddaughter. Well, she's rich and I'm not.'

Roland gave an incredulous chortle. 'Oh, I can't believe Liam would think that! Why should he?'

Carly had imagined she could sit and look straight at him and relate the whole story, but she found it easier to look across the room or down at her plate. For all her gaiety she had a deep reserve, and she had been savagely humiliated in that courtroom and by Gerald's conduct. She didn't know which had cut deeper, the pitiless questioning or the way Gerald had tried to blame her, but she didn't want anyone looking into her eyes while she was talking about it.

She said quietly, 'I had seen Liam before. Nearly four years ago when I lived up North I met a man, a student, and we went around together. He said his father was a banker, he seemed to have money to burn. But his father was a bank clerk and Gerald was stealing the money.'

'And Liam——' Roland's voice rose in hushed horror, he was wondering if Liam might have prosecuted her, and she said quickly,

'It wasn't his case. Gerald's counsel was a friend of his and he was in the public gallery. And I wasn't in the dock, I was in the witness box. I hadn't a clue I was wearing stolen jewellery, or helping to spend stolen money, but I admit it sounded bad, and your brother has me down as someone not over-bothered by scruples.'

Roland took a sip of brandy and coughed on it, and Carly knew that this had thrown him. 'It isn't like Liam to be prejudiced,' he said. He was apologising for his brother, but she felt that he respected Liam's judgment and was usually influenced by it, and she smiled, 'So do please thank your aunt, but tell her I can't get away at the moment. Some other time, perhaps.'

Roland had the grace to flush. 'I'm sorry. You don't think I believe that you'd do Aunt Aimée anything but good? If you don't come she's going to be terribly disappointed, and so am I. I'm counting on it. Surely you

can manage a week or two. Better still, a few weeks.'
He was over his embarrassment before the end of that
speech, and when Carly still hesitated he said, 'She'll
be hurt if you turn her hospitality down. I can promise
you a good holiday. Do you ride?'

'No.'

'I'll teach you.' The white teeth flashed. 'Don't you
want to sleep in Napoleon's bed?'

'Honestly?'

'Cross my heart. And any lessons you need there——
——' he leered engagingly, and it was nice to laugh. It
dispersed the darkness and brought her back to this
brightly lit hotel dining room, and Roland, who
believed she could be trusted, even if Liam didn't.

'I'll be sure to let you know,' she said, spearing a
strawberry from the top of her gâteau, 'but I wouldn't
advise you to count on it.'

Ruth was watching the late-night movie when Carly
got back. 'I liked this one,' said Ruth.

'An improvement on the other, isn't he?' Roland had
just kissed her goodnight at the front door, and Carly's
lips felt warm and soft.

'Much cosier,' said Ruth. They had only talked
briefly before Carly went out on her date, but Ruth
felt at ease with Roland, while Liam had scared her
half to death. 'Did he say anything about going to
Brittany?'

'If you can fix up some help in the shop. I'm booking
a flight some time next week, and Roland's meeting
me at Rouen.'

'It's so romantic,' sighed Ruth. 'It all sounds like
something out of a novel.'

Carly was smiling with closed lips, and Ruth thought
she was dreaming of Roland, waiting for her when she

stepped off that plane. But the man in Carly's mind was Liam. She was imagining how he would feel when Roland told him that Caroline Brown was on her way to the Château des Sables.

She rather expected Liam to turn up again. Either that or phone, after he had warned her so bluntly to keep away from Madame Corbé. Roland rang the following afternoon to ask her if she would like him to book her flight ticket and she said firmly, 'Thank you, but I'll get it. It's no trouble. I know the girl in the travel agency.' She wasn't having Liam deciding she was sponging already. She spoke to Madame Corbé, who sounded as though Carly was doing her the favour, and made her promise to follow on the very first flight she could. 'And you'll come and dine with us here on Friday night, won't you?'

'I suppose you couldn't come to us?' Carly suggested. There would be no risk of Liam Sherrard joining that party, but as Madame Corbé pointed out, she and Roland were leaving quite early next day, so it would be more convenient for her if Carly could dine with them. 'Yes, of course,' said Carly. 'Thank you, I'd like to come.' It was left that Roland should collect her on Friday, and in the meantime she would book her ticket just as soon as she knew for certain that Ruth could manage in her absence.

That afternoon Ruth spoke to the mothers waiting outside school to collect their children while she was waiting for William, and found two who were willing to help in the shop. 'I can manage,' Ruth announced over tea that evening. 'You can't let a chance like this slip by.' The chance of a wonderful holiday, she meant, although she was probably wondering if maybe, just maybe, this wealthy family that Carly had stumbled on might invest a little money in a little shop.

Carly hoped she wasn't. The thought had crossed her own mind, but not since meeting Liam. He wouldn't believe it was a business proposition, he'd think it was a con trick. 'I'll see that you don't get a penny out of Madame Corbé,' he'd said, so she'd see to it that she never asked for a penny.

If she had taken him up on his offer to buy her off she might have suggested he buy the lease. As a lump sum that would have been high, so it would have depended on how much of a threat he thought she was, and if she could have stomached being a blackmailer. She couldn't, of course. Life would be simpler without scruples, but ever since Gerald Carly had never put herself in any man's debt, and she would have to be very desperate indeed before she would accept anything at all from Liam Sherrard.

She got a ticket for a week the following Thursday, and began working furiously to finish some of the uncompleted garments in the sewing room. She took her machine into the shop during the day, in the van, so that no time was wasted, and worked at home in the evenings, cutting out all dates. She couldn't help feeling a little guilty, dashing off on holiday, although she hadn't had a holiday this year.

Barney phoned and she said she couldn't see him, explaining, 'I'm going to France for a couple of weeks. It's all a heck of a rush, but an offer came up that I can't turn down, from a very nice old lady who came into the shop. She lives in Brittany and she's invited me to her home for a fortnight.'

'A holiday with a nice old lady?' he jeered. 'What as? Companion-nurse?'

'I'll send you a postcard,' she said.

'When are you going?'

'A week today.'

'Where from?'

'Birmingham.'

'Can I run you to the airport?' he offered.

'Thank you very much,' said Carly.

Friday evening was the only night she was going out and she wasn't looking forward to visiting Liam Sherrard's house again. She wondered if he had told Madame Corbé about Gerald or if—which would be worse—he might refer to the case over the meal. Hints, or digs, to keep Carly in a state of apprehension. If he tried that she would come right out with it, look right at him and ask, 'Does your aunt know where we saw each other before?'

'How did Liam take the news that I'm accepting your aunt's invitation?' she asked Roland, as she sat beside him in his car, speeding towards Liam's house.

He kept his eyes on the road and his voice casual. 'He just reminded Aunt Aimée, "So long as you remember that she isn't Antoinette".'

That was sound advice, it was something Carly must emphasise herself, but she doubted if that was all Liam had said. 'And?' she prompted.

'Aunt Aimée's a shrewd old bird,' said Roland slowly, as though he would rather have left this out. 'She said, "You don't like her, do you?" and Liam said, "Not my type".'

'And that's all?'

'Hardly a compliment,' said Roland, 'but he was quite amiable about it.'

Oh no! thought Carly. She was positive that Liam Sherrard was not amiable, nor resigned to the situation. He had walked out on her, white with anger. He thought she was dangerous and she knew he was.

She made herself laugh, 'So tell me, what is his type?' and Roland named a well-known model and a duke's daughter, and chuckled, 'Among others.'

'Among others?' Carly echoed. 'Does your brother get jilted a lot?'

'Not at all,' said Roland cheerfully. 'But he doesn't believe in marriage, so he keeps on the move.'

'You mean women actually want to *marry* him?' She gurgled incredulously. 'What *do* they see in him?'

'I don't know,' said Roland, 'but I've been waiting for years for some girl to ask that. Are you shortsighted, by the way?'

'Forty-forty vision,' quipped Carly blithely. 'I suppose he's just not my type,' and they laughed together, and she wouldn't have admitted for the world that her flippancy was hiding a feeling of dread at the prospect of another encounter with Liam.

Madame Corbé was sitting at a bureau in the drawing room when Roland and Carly walked into the room. She had been writing a letter, but she pushed it aside with a little cry of welcome, got up and came to meet them, putting her arms around Carly. 'It's lovely to see you,' she smiled.

She was not normally a demonstrative woman. Carly hadn't seen her embrace any of her birthday guests like this. When Liam's girl-friend had tried to hug her she had held back, offering a cool cheek, but this was like a family welcome, and Carly felt that Liam would not have approved at all.

There was no sign of Liam. As she had stepped into the hall Carly had looked for him, from door to door, up to the landing of the staircase; and in this room her glance had swept wide before she was reassured that

Madame Corbé was alone.

She couldn't ask about him. She sat beside Madame Corbé and chattered about some of the customers who had come into the shop that week, embroidering incidents to make them funnier or more interesting. But it wasn't until they went into the dining room—where only three places were laid—that she breathed freely. Liam wasn't eating with them, and that meant Carly would be able to get down her food without fighting a tightness in her throat.

'Liam can't be with us,' said Madame Corbé, as though she had noticed Carly counting places. 'He's working late. But I do hope he'll be back before you go.'

That's me for an early night, thought Carly, smiling and saying nothing, although Roland laughed. 'It's all right, Aunt Aimée, Carly knows she's not his type.'

Madame Corbé looked blank. 'Indeed?' then seated herself and began to serve the soup.

Released from the strain of waiting for Liam, Carly relaxed and had a very pleasant evening. The more she saw of Madame Corbé the more she liked her. It had nothing to do with money, as Liam had suggested. She had felt the same when she had imagined Madame Corbé was hard up and alone, and after dinner she sat beside the old lady on a green velvet sofa, talking, listening, so that Roland, in an armchair on the other side of the fireplace, seemed the odd man out.

When a clock struck eleven Madame Corbé said, 'Surely Liam can't be much longer,' and Carly jumped.

'It's never that late! I must go. You've a long day ahead of you tomorrow, a long journey. It's been a lovely evening.'

She couldn't believe how the time had flown. She would be seeing Madame Corbé again next week she said, and she was looking forward to that very much indeed. Madame Corbé kissed her and said, 'Take care, child,' and went with them to the door.

As Carly settled into the passenger seat of his car Roland observed, 'You've got a gift for it.'

'A gift for what?'

'Getting on with people. I've never seen Aunt Aimée take to anybody before the way she's taken to you.'

'Do you mind?' She would hate Roland to share Liam's suspicions about her because she liked Roland. But he smiled and bent his head to kiss her cheek, assuring her,

'Of course I don't mind. She's showing very good taste.' The headlights of a car drawing up behind flashed in the rear-view mirror and he turned and announced, 'It's Liam. Do you want to say goodnight?'

'I don't want to say anything,' she said quickly. 'Please let's go.'

Roland's car drew away, and Carly waved to Madame Corbé who was still standing silhouetted in the doorway. Then she looked back, watching the headlights until she was quite sure Liam Sherrard was not following them. She had made her getaway in the nick of time, because two minutes with him could have spoiled the whole evening for her.

'I'll be waiting for you on Thursday,' said Roland, when he delivered her home.

'I'll be looking for you,' she said, and the lamplight put shadows in his face, hollowing his cheekbones, and giving him a faint resemblance to his brother.

'You're shivering,' he said. He was kissing her goodnight, under the lamp-post just outside Ruth's house, and she said, 'It's turned cold,' but she was shivering because she had imagined Liam's face just above hers, and Liam's hard arms holding her. . . .

She couldn't believe that Liam would let her leave on that holiday without another word. Every time the phone rang in the days that followed her muscles tensed. He was so vividly in her mind that she felt haunted. She 'saw' him walking on the other side of the road, only it wasn't him, it was just another tall man. She suspected she was dreaming about him, because although she didn't remember her dreams she kept waking in the morning feeling anxious, and that was something that hadn't happened to her for a long time.

On Wednesday evening she was washing her hair when Ruth put her head round the bathroom door and said, 'Caller for you,' and Carly croaked, 'Is it Liam?'

'No,' said Ruth. 'It's Lucy from next door. She wants you to bring her some duty-free scent. Were you expecting Liam?'

'Not really,' said Carly, but she couldn't rid herself of the fear that even now he would find some way to stop her leaving.

'You can do with this holiday,' said Ruth, nodding wisely. 'You're looking tired,' and Carly thought, that isn't exhaustion, that's strain. She had been on a razor's edge ever since she first saw Liam at the birthday party, but his time was running out. She would be away early in the morning and once at the airport all she would have to do was let the plane carry her to Rouen where Roland would be waiting for her—Rouen, so that he could spend a day or so showing her something of Normandy as well.

Barney arrived, as he'd promised, to drive her to the

airport. The alarm clock had failed to ring, and the last
twenty-five minutes had been hectic with Carly dashing around, getting dressed, making up, and finishing
last-minute packing; while Ruth brewed tea and
cooked bacon and egg and urged Carly to eat.

'You must have something before you set off,' Ruth
insisted, and when Carly shrieked, 'I haven't *time!*' she
made the bacon into a sandwich and followed Carly
round with it. So that instead of leaving the house
looking composed and elegant Carly tumbled into
Barney's car clutching a bacon sandwich, and collapsed
in the seat, letting her head fall back. 'The alarm didn't
go off,' she told him. 'Dratted thing. I must have
pressed the wrong button.'

He had loaded her case in the trunk. 'We're in
plenty of time,' he said reassuringly and she smiled at
him.

'Thank you for the lift.'

She was flushed from the rush, pink-cheeked, and
Barney wished he was going with her. There was
something so alive and vibrant about Carly. 'Who is
this old woman you're staying with?' he asked.

'Madame Corbé. I told you she was living in
Brittany. Guirec Vert it's called, the place.' She was
going on to tell him about the birthday party and perhaps Roland. Not about Liam. She didn't want to talk
about Liam to anybody. But Barney was frowning
slightly, and if he turned jealous and refused to drive
her to Birmingham she was going to have a job getting
a taxi, and no hope of a bus or train. The old van
probably wouldn't make it and it would be ironic if
she failed to reach Rouen through her own stupid
fault.

She said, 'She has an estate out there and she's a

very nice lady. I suppose you don't fancy a bacon sandwich?'

Barney's expression was queasy, and Carly took a mouthful of congealing bread and bacon, then hastily wrapped the rest in a tissue and put it in her pocket, and asked if he'd heard the weather forecast because flying in windy weather made her nervous.

They made good speed, the radio playing music, with time checks and news bulletins; and Barney moaning about the news. Carly felt cocooned in pleasurable anticipation. She was the one off on holiday, he was being left behind, and she could understand him being niggly, although he took half a dozen holidays to her one and she never begrudged him his higher standard of living.

She sat back, drowsy in the warm car, and when he asked 'Have you thought any more about moving in with me?' she yawned.

'It wouldn't work.'

'I think it would.' He thought she would look like this at breakfast, in the mornings, sleepy-eyed and flushed, her hair tumbled, and that it would be pleasant to have the right to reach out for her because she was committed to him. But perhaps this was not the time to urge her to make a decision. When she came back from what sounded like a luxurious holiday the little terraced house might be less appealing than his apartment.

At the airport they checked in her luggage, then sat down in the main lounge and waited for the flight to be called. Carly was anxious to be away. She hadn't had a real holiday for a long time, and although she was grateful to Barney for the lift she wished now that he would leave her. She would have enjoyed buying herself a book, although she had said she didn't want anything to read when he'd suggested getting her a magazine. She might have gone into the coffee lounge. She would have liked to wander about and savour the excitement of an airport.

But Barney hung on, and said, 'No hurry,' when she said, 'Thank you very much for bringing me, I'm fine now if you should be anywhere else.' So they sat together, and he told her how much he was going to miss her and she said, 'I'll be back,' and when her flight was called jumped eagerly to her feet.

He got up too, and said, 'Think about it while you're away. Moving in with me.' His hands were on her shoulders and he drew her closer and kissed her soundly, and over his shoulder Carly saw the tall figure of Liam Sherrard unfold from the lounge seat that had been backing on theirs, and she froze as he walked round and stood, smiling at them.

'They've called our flight,' he said, and Barney loosed her, whirled round and stared. Liam Sherrard looked successful in the understated way that took it all for granted. He had the assurance and charisma that Barney wanted and envied, and Carly wished she could say, 'You're much nicer,' but Barney was sneering, 'So this is the offer you couldn't refuse?'

He thought she had planned to go with Liam, which was stupid, because if she had she wouldn't have let Barney bring her to the airport, telling him a tale about holidaying with an old lady.

'When you've finished saying goodbye to your friend,' said Liam affably, and she tried to explain,

'This is Madame Corbé's nephew——'

'The one you forgot to mention?' Barney glared at Liam with a brooding resentment, then turned on his heel and went down the stairs so fast that he was at the bottom before Carly could think of a way to call him back.

Actually there was no way, and she had this strange feeling that everything was turning muzzy around her, that only Liam Sherrard stood clear and hard, his fingers on her elbow biting deep. The fact that he had materialised in flesh and blood was almost a relief. She had been running from shadows all week, but ever since that first night she had expected him to reappear.

Barney had no claim on her, but she hadn't wanted this to happen, and she might have run after him if there had been time, and Liam hadn't been marching her towards the checkpoint.

They went through, proffering passports, then tickets, and she snapped, 'You must have gone to a lot of trouble getting this flight.'

'Not a lot.'

'What for?'

'I've a few days to play around with and I told you I was going to keep an eye on you. This will give us time to get to know each other.' His eyes gleamed wickedly, and there were those who might say he was loaded with charm, but Carly was not among them. And all the time she had this feeling that the moving crowds were almost dreamlike. It was getting up early and having no breakfast. It was the jolting shock of finding him there.

Liam stood aside to let her climb the steps into the plane and she didn't want to sit beside him, but there she was, in the window seat, and he was next to her, blocking any escape into the aisle. She turned her head stiffly and met his gaze, trying to see him impersonally, and realised how extremely good-looking he was—fine-boned, with a beautiful cruel mouth, a slightly hooked nose. Roland, like Barney, like most of her men friends, was a man of today. Their appearance was right for the times, but Liam. Sherrard would have been a knock-out in any century. She could imagine him in Roman times, wearing a toga, or in a wig and velvet jacket conversing with Voltaire.

He was watching her, unblinkingly, and after that she looked past him at the other passengers, as intently as though she expected to recognise a face. It kept her eyes off Liam and as the plane rose she watched the airport slipping away beneath them.

Barney was down there. She hoped he wouldn't drive stupidly because he was still annoyed. He thought she was off on holiday with Liam, and that was so absurd that her lips twitched and Liam asked, 'Who is he?'

No business of yours, she thought, but she said, 'A friend who gave me a lift.' He had been listening to their conversation, so he knew, so she added, 'And who wants me to move in with him.'

'But you won't.' He wasn't asking a question. He said it as though that was settled, and Carly asked,

'How do you know?'

Liam shrugged wide shoulders under the beautifully cut jacket, 'Because a better offer has come up,' and she breathed deeply, fighting for self-control, until she reckoned that she could manage to sound calm.

'Look,' she said, 'I like flying, and I had hoped to enjoy this flight. But the only way I can do it is by pretending you're not here so would you just shut up? Please.'

Then she looked out of the window again, keeping her face resolutely turned away, but she was still agonisingly conscious of him. She was sure that Liam was sitting comfortably in his seat, relaxed, eyes closed probably. But after a while the crick in her neck had spread into an ache running up into her skull. If she stayed this tense she was going to be paralysed by Rouen. They'd have to carry her out. She rubbed the nape of her neck, under the heavy fall of her hair, then stretched a little in her seat and said, 'I feel like a prisoner with a jailer.' Then she bit her lip hard because that would make him remember Gerald.

He was so close to her that she could feel him. He wasn't touching her, but his nearness was a pressure: his arm on the armrest, the lean muscles in his thighs, the long legs. Carly shifted uncomfortably and asked, 'How long before we get there?'

'Three quarters of an hour to Rouen,' he said. 'Then about another two hundred and fifty miles to Guirec Vert.'

'But Roland's meeting me at Rouen?' She had taken that for granted, but now that Liam had turned up she was beginning to wonder. He shook his head slowly and she shook hers faster, trying to deny what he was telling her. 'He *isn't*? There'll be just *you*?'

'How many escorts do you need?' He sounded amused, but if he was going to be her sole companion all the way to Brittany she didn't think she could stand it. Not feeling like this, aching with tension. She said desperately,

'Maybe we could pretend we just met. Forget our first meeting—and our last. Be civil.'

'Why not?' If she hadn't known that he disliked and distrusted her she might have found him attractive when he smiled. He said, as though he was making conversation with a stranger, 'Going on holiday, are you?'

'Yes. Yes, I am. To a place called Güirec Vert. Would you have heard of it?'

'You don't say?' He feigned astonishment. 'Small world. I was practically brought up there.'

'Really? My, my! Do your family live there?'

Talking over dinner the day after the birthday party Roland had told her that Madame Corbé was the only relative he and Liam had. 'They do,' said Liam. 'And where do your parents live?'

Carly said, 'I don't know, I never did,' and in the silence that followed she noticed what long lashes he had, the colour of his eyes—grey with dark flecks— and felt her heart leap and began to babble, 'Actually it isn't true that I love flying. Really it scares me rigid. I haven't done much, but I did go on this package tour the year before last and the wheels stuck up when we should have been coming down and we were circling Palma airport for the best part of an hour.'

'I'm glad you landed safely,' he said.

'Are you really?'

'Very glad, and now you need some Dutch courage, like a large brandy.' He signalled the air hostess, who came dashing up, showing pretty teeth in a sexy way that was all for Liam's benefit. But he kept looking at Carly. 'Drink up,' he ordered, and she took a sip and asked,

'Do you fly a lot?'

'A fair amount.'

'If we start diving can I grab you?' She was joking, but when Liam said,

'Any time at all,' she could feel his warmth and his touch.

'Thanks,' she said, 'that makes me feel safer.'

She was feeling safer, and it had nothing to do with

the brandy. It was because the man sitting beside her had stopped being her jailer. She wished he didn't have that memory of her in the courtroom, but he had said this journey would give them a chance to get to know each other, and it was suddenly important that he should know and understand.

She said, 'I probably wouldn't be on this plane if you hadn't gone round to Ruth's. I really shouldn't be taking a holiday right now, but you made me so mad that I had to come.'

'So I defeated my object?' His grin was engaging.

'Yes.' She would have been pleased to be asked and she would have tried to visit Madame Corbé and Roland some time, but all this urgency was only to show Liam that he couldn't bully her. 'Roland said you're not usually prejudiced,' and she looked straight at him. 'Did you just make an exception in my case?'

'I probably did,' he said quietly, and the admission encouraged her to go on.

'Truly I didn't know about Gerald. He said he was rich and I believed him. It was lovely being spoiled, I never had been, and he bought me things and I let him. But I wouldn't have done, God knows, if I'd any idea. I'm not a taker. I wouldn't take a thing from Madame Corbé. I like her very much and I wish I was her granddaughter, but, like you said, under the skin there wouldn't be much Antoinette and I had in common.'

Liam gave a small nod, agreeing, but there was no harshness in his face now, and when she said, 'So you don't have to worry, I won't be plotting to get my hands on the family silver,' they both smiled, and it was surely a truce.

As they walked from the Customs at Rouen she said,

quite happily, 'This wasn't how I thought it was going to be.'

She had expected to have Roland hurrying to meet her, not Liam striding beside her. 'He's trusting you with me,' said Liam, and she laughed.

'You can be trusted?'

'Most of the time.'

Carly added mischievously, 'Well, Victoria seems to have faith in you. I wonder she didn't come along.' When she thought about it she had wondered very much, because most of the time at that party Miss Victoria Hayden had been hanging on to Liam like a limpet.

'She wasn't asked,' he said cheerfully. 'Not by Aunt Aimée, and it is Aunt Aimée's house.'

She wasn't sorry about that. She supposed she was sorry that Roland wasn't here to meet them, but it was a long way to come and unnecessary when Liam was travelling the same road. Now they were letting bygones be bygones she didn't mind travelling with Liam. She was not surprised to see the car waiting, he would have everything organised in style, and all she had to do was get in and sit back. Which she did, with shining eyes because it was a beautiful day and she felt wonderful, ready for anything, as though she was off on some mind-blowing, breathtaking adventure.

The sunshine roof was open, a warm breeze blew through her hair, and she said blissfully, 'It's a wonderful life, isn't it? Right now isn't it a wonderful life?'

'Right now it surely is.' Liam's hair was ruffled and he seemed another man from the one who had looked at her with granite-hard eyes and told her he would knock her down if she should be rash enough to hit out at him. Years younger, for one thing. 'You're dead set on making for the Château?' he asked. Carly stiffened for a second, then realised they weren't taking that corner on the wrong side, this was the right side. 'You wouldn't rather have Paris?' he said.

He was joking, of course, and she grinned, 'Are you kidnapping me?'

'It's a nice day for kidnapping.'

'Better not,' she said, but she thought, it would be fun if we could go anywhere, stop any place.

'Where would you like to eat?' he asked her. 'There's a guidebook in there,' he nodded towards the glove compartment in front of her. 'And a map. Can you read a map?'

'Of course,' she said airily. 'I'm very partial to a map. But what I'd really like to do is buy some food and eat out of doors—have a picnic. Would you mind doing that?'

It was market day in the little town where they stopped. Stalls filled the square, but they managed to park in a side street and went shopping for their lunch. From the charcuterie they bought cheese and quiches and pâté and butter, and a bottle of red wine, and from the pâtisserie a long crusty loaf and raspberry-filled fruit tarts.

Liam spoke colloquial French so fast that Carly, hanging back, could only follow a word here and there. No one took him for a tourist; she supposed he wasn't if he had been practically reared here. He had left his coat in the car and in shirtsleeves he looked at home. They bought cheap glass tumblers, paper plates and plastic knives, dropping them into a carrier bag, and wandered through the market, adding a melon.

The buildings round the square were tall, half-timbered, with paintwork peeling, but picturesque and

mysterious with closed shutters and narrow little alley-
ways.

When they left the bustle of the market square and
wandered down the cobbled side streets Liam took her
hand, his fingers twining with hers, because it was a
natural thing to do when the sun was shining and they
were strolling together. She liked the feel of this to-
getherness. There seemed to be something familiar
and sweet about it. When he squeezed her hand tighter
for a moment, and smiled at her, her breath caught as
though he had kissed her lips, and she felt a quickening
of real desire. It wasn't just that Liam had sex appeal,
more as though they had been together for a long time
and knew each other so well that a smile and a hand
pressure conveyed a silent message.

If I believed in reincarnation, she thought, that could
explain why I'm feeling weak at the knees now, as if
my body knows your lovemaking. But a likelier explanation was mutual physical attraction, and the fact
that, right now, he and she were on the same wave-
length of makebelieve.

A poster in one of the windows said, '*A Vendre*',
and Liam followed her glance and said, 'Shall we look
at it?'

Carly pretended to consider, then shook her head.
'Too pricey,' she said, as though she had walked this
way before, and knew house values here, and that had
been a serious suggestion. And she thought what a
narrow division there was between fact and fantasy,
because she could imagine so easily that they were
going home together to a little room above a street like
this, carrying their food for tonight.

There was a café on the corner, with tables filling
the pavement. 'Coffee?' he suggested.

'Uh-huh,' and they sat down, ordering big cups of strong coffee. She noticed how almost all the women gave Liam a second glance, how the girl who served them had fluffed up her hair between taking their order and bringing it, and grinned, and Liam asked, 'What are you smiling at?'

'The waitress fancies you,' she said, and he grinned back.

'That's all right, then. I thought you were ogling that character over there who's staring pop-eyed at you.'

Carly looked across and caught the eye of a sandy-haired young man at an adjoining table. He was staring at her. Men often did, and she rarely took any notice. He looked sheepish as she smiled, then started to smile too until Liam veered round.

Carly swallowed laughter at Liam's ferocious scowl. It made him look as though his next move would be to swagger over and push in the inoffensive face of her admirer, who looked hastily away, then drained his glass and hurried off.

'Now who asked you to do that?' she asked, her lips twitching. 'What harm was the poor man doing? Do you see me telling the waitress to shove off?'

'You can't very well, can you?' Liam pointed out. 'She works here—probably owns it. You look good enough to eat, you know, I don't blame him.' She had left her jacket behind in the car too. Her shirt was scoop-necked and sleeveless and her skin was pale honey in the sunshine. 'Like an apricot,' added Liam.

'I'm starving,' said Carly, and she was, any moment her stomach was going to start rumbling.

'Shall we eat here?'

They were serving bowls of soup, quiches and

patés, but she said, 'I was promised a picnic, you're not suggesting wasting all that stuff in there, I hope?'

About half an hour out of town they found the ideal spot, soft turf backed by trees, drew the car off the road and emptied their carrier bag. It all tasted wonderful. They drank from the thick tumblers, tearing the fresh crusty bread apart with their fingers and spreading it thick with butter and pâté. They sat on the turf, Liam leaning against a tree trunk, Carly, towards the end of the meal, leaning on him.

It was quite incredible that he was the same man she had faced in Ruth's little front room, whose guts she had hated. She was eating melon and so was he, his face masked by the half-moon rind, and she sat back and goggled in astonishment. 'You are Liam, aren't you? There isn't another brother? Twins? You are Roland's one and only, the lawyer?'

'That's me.'

'Did you always want to be a lawyer?' It was in the family, Roland had said the ones with the brains went into law, but Liam would probably have been a success at anything he attempted, and Carly wondered if he had ever had other dreams.

'Oh yes,' he said. 'What about you? What did you want to be?'

Somebody's child. That had been her first dream, a real name, not one that had been given to her like a number. They hadn't shown much imagination with 'Brown' and nobody seemed to know why 'Caroline'. She dropped her melon rind back in the bag and wiped her sticky fingers with a cleansing pad. 'I like what I do,' she said, 'making clothes.'

'How did you start?'

'I always liked sewing. After I left the orphanage I

made most of my own clothes and then I wondered about doing it professionally. I was a salesgirl when I met Gerald and after—all that—I wanted to get away, and I fancied some sort of career, so I took this course in design and dressmaking.'

It had brought her to the Midlands. She had completed it and was earning her living as a waitress in a Stratford hotel, preparing her first 'collection' to take round the shops, when she'd met Ruth. She told Liam all this, she seemed to be doing all the talking. He put in a word here and there, and they got on with the meal until the bottle of wine was almost empty and most of the food had gone, and Carly started to pack away the debris into the carrier bag.

Then she remembered the sandwich still in her coat pocket and brought that out. 'Bacon sandwich,' she explained. 'Ruth made it. It was supposed to be my breakfast.'

'For dinner,' said Liam, 'you shall have a superb meal.' He was still leaning against the tree trunk, long legs crossed at the ankles, hands clasped behind his head. He breathed deeply as though savouring a superb aroma. 'Marvellous,' he said. 'A legend in its own time.'

'What is?' Carly eyed him quizzically. 'You look too thin to care about food,' and he grinned.

'Just selective in my appetites, but ravenous for the best.'

She burst out laughing. 'So what's a legend in its own time?'

'The hotel we should reach about seven this evening.' He checked his watch. 'So long as we leave here in the next hour or so.'

'When do we reach the Château?'

'Again, it depends when we set off. Early tomorrow evening, I should think.'

She had known it was a long run, and she had known they were taking their time, but she had presumed they were making straight for Guirec Vert with no overnight stop on the way. She was holding the wine bottle and as she put it into the carrier among the papers and scraps she asked, 'Do your aunt and Roland know we won't be arriving till tomorrow?'

'Of course.'

He sounded positive enough, and she looked down at him, unconvinced but undecided what she should do, biting her lower lip thoughtfully.

CHAPTER FOUR

THEY came to L'Auberge des Deux Soeurs as night was falling, with stars already thick in the sky. The air was soft, and seemed scented to Carly. She thought it was roses, that were in a garden somewhere, but the courtyard where they drew up alongside a row of parked cars was high-walled and dominated by the big sprawling outline of the inn.

It had been a farmhouse, Liam had told her, driving along. After the war two widowed sisters had started a restaurant, which had prospered until now it was an hotel where the food and service and standard of comfort brought customers back again and again.

Another couple were walking across the courtyard ahead of them, and the entrance hall was pleasantly full. Not crowded, but enough people to tell you that the place was popular, all looking as though they were enjoying their evening out. Through an archway Carly saw the dining room—red flock wallpaper, white tablecloths, the gleam of silver—and behind the mahogany desk a woman with grey hair done in a bun, wearing a grey silk blouse and a large cameo brooch, greeted Liam like an old friend.

This was Madame Marie, one of the sisters. There were three generations helping to run the inn now, and Carly wondered how long Liam had been coming. The man who picked up their cases looked in his mid-thirties, and he said he was enchanted to meet Carly and then went on talking in French to Liam. As they followed him upstairs he asked about Madame Corbé's health—she got that, but the rest was gibberish to her.

He stopped on the first floor, opening a door, and this was her room. There were two rooms waiting. 'If we are staying somewhere overnight I want my own room,' she had said, sitting on the turf under the trees when Liam broke the news that they were ending the day here. 'And so you shall,' he had said. But she had still watched closely when Madame took down the keys. If only one had been produced she would probably have made a stand, although the booking must have been made before Liam left England, and the way things were then he could hardly have presumed on sharing a room or anything else with Carly.

The room was delightful—shell pink, with looped curtains and frills around the bed and dressing table. She peered into the tiny bathroom, which was palest pink too. She needed a bath. As soon as she had unpacked she would go in there and float away the grime of the day.

The other door obviously led into an adjoining room. Carly slid the bolt and tapped, hearing a bolt slide on the other side, then the door opened and Liam said, 'Hello.'

'They must be used to you bringing ladies along.'

'Believe it or not,' he said, 'they thought the second room was booked for my aunt.'

'Then why the connecting door?'

'When she's sleeping in strange beds she likes someone within call.'

She didn't believe him, but it was a good try. 'Well, I'm in very good health,' she said lightly, 'so we can shut the door, because if I want to get in touch I'll manage to walk over and knock.'

'Any time,' he said, and again she had the feeling that this was familiar, she and Liam standing close, no doors locked between them, only the rest of the world locked out. 'Any time at all,' he added, and Carly put hands up to cheeks that were suddenly hot, and turned to look around her room.

'It's so pretty that I don't feel I should be walking around in it looking grubby and sticky.'

'You look beautiful.' His voice was husky, as if that wasn't just a simple compliment but almost as though he was saying, 'I think I'm falling in love with you.' Then he smiled, 'You want a bath, you want your dinner. See you downstairs in half an hour?'

'Mmm.' She got that out and managed a smile, and she thought she was the one who shut the door. But Liam might have done, because she didn't believe she would have turned away before she had said that she wanted a bath and she wanted her dinner, but most of all she wanted him.

It was as well the door was closed, because that

would have been right out of character. Carly was always the one who held back. She never rushed into an affair, and she was glad now that she had half an hour to collect herself. Besides, she was looking a mess, although Liam had said she was beautiful.

She opened her case, unpacked nightclothes and took out her favourite dress. She hadn't made this one, she had bought it in a rash moment of extravagance and always felt wicked and wonderful in it. It was in bronze lamé, cut straight across the bust, with thin shoulder straps. The long straight skirt had a high side slit and she wore it with a gilt tube necklace and a smooth bronze bangle. After she had let slip how much she had paid for it it became Barney's favourite too. If they were likely to meet anyone he wanted to impress he would often say, 'Wear your little glitter dress.'

She hoped Barney was all right. She hadn't given him another thought since Birmingham airport vanished in the mists, and after that fleeting reflection he slipped out of her mind again.

In this dress, and after she had bathed and put on her make-up, she should look as fetching as most of the ladies Liam Sherrard had travelled with. Carly knew her good points, she had had to shift for herself, and she had learned how to make the best of her appearance. When she went downstairs she intended to look stunning.

There was a bath sachet in the bathroom and she swished up the water to a foamy pale green, then undressed quickly and slid beneath the foam line with a shiver of delight. A pity she couldn't let her head fall back and her hair float out on the water—but there was no time for washing her hair, nor really for lying and soaking, although this was wonderfully comforting.

If Ruth could see me now, she thought, and know who's in the next room shaving and showering and getting ready to have dinner with me and tell me again that I'm beautiful.

Liam was beautiful, he really was. She raised a leg, stretching her toes and watching the water cascade off; and she could imagine Liam beneath the shower, dark hair flattened as water streamed over his head and shoulders and in rivulets down the slim muscular body with his broad shoulders and flat stomach.

'I am beautiful,' she said. She had long, long legs and a good figure. Men desired her. She was fairly sure that Liam wanted her, and she was quite sure that thinking about him stirred a need in her that was almost frightening.

She towelled herself dry and looked at her face in the mirror over the handbasin and said, 'No, I'm not.' Not beautiful, but she could still look good enough to eat, as he'd said while they were drinking their coffee; and there was a radiance about her now that made her satisfied with her appearance when she was dressed and ready to go downstairs.

She had taken a few minutes over the half hour. The corridor was empty when she stepped out of her room, the voices and the laughter were all coming from the ground floor, and when she reached the top of the staircase she looked down on the entrance hall. Liam was sitting at a table by a window talking to a man and a woman, but almost immediately he looked up.

Her moving figure at the top of the stairs must have caught his eye, of course he was expecting her to appear, but she thought, I saw you right away, I didn't look around for you, and the moment I saw you you saw me. How about that?

He said a few words to his companions and came to the bottom of the stairs, and Carly walked down with her inborn grace, head high, smiling. 'Hello,' she said, and he took her hand for the last step and her skin tingled.

He wore black slacks and a midnight blue velvet jacket, and his shirt was fine lawn. His hair was still damp so that it curled slightly round his ears and at the nape of his neck. 'Every time I see you,' she said, 'you look different. I suppose it *is* the clothes?'

He grinned, 'There's one way of finding out,' and she raised her eyebrows.

'Oh, I don't think they'd care for any stripping off in the foyer. We'd never get our dinner after that.'

She felt quite crazily happy, as though she had drunk a lot of champagne or won the pools or found herself in Paradise. 'How do I look?' she asked, as Liam guided her towards the archway leading to the dining room, and he said, 'Fantastic. And very expensive. You never made that dress?'

'You're right,' she said, 'I never did.'

They were seated by the young woman who came to meet them and who chattered volubly in French to Liam, all the way down the dining room—at a table for two in an alcove, and presented with menus, hand-written in beautiful script.

There was discussion between Liam and the young woman, during which Carly listened, looking from one to the other, and when Liam asked her, 'What do you think?' she shrugged,

'Not a lot, I can't understand what you're saying.'

'Sorry.' He began to translate, and she said,

'I'll go along with what you're having. I'm sure it's going to be delicious.' The surprise would be part of the fun. Everything that had happened to her since she had stepped into that plane had been unplanned. For years she had managed her life. The episode with Gerald had made her cautious, but this was a holiday, without responsibilities or cares, and she knew that whatever Liam selected would be good.

She was right. The food from the kitchen of the Inn of the Two Sisters was out of this world. The soup was superb, then fillets of sole Mornay and veal chops with truffles.

It was the best meal Carly had ever eaten, and Liam Sherrard was probably the most attractive man with whom she had ever shared a table for two. Certainly he was the most intelligent. He told her about his work, and had her laughing at some of the cases and characters he had come across, and she talked about the boutique.

'You do all right?' he asked. 'Well, I'm sure you do. It looks a very attractive shop, I'm sure the customers flock in.'

'You've seen it?' Carly was slightly surprised, but he explained,

'My aunt's talked about it. She was very impressed.'

'She seemed to like sitting there and watching,' Carly admitted. 'And yes, it is a nice little shop.'

She speared a tiny morsel of truffle and chewed it slowly, serious for the moment, then shook the gravity off and smiled, 'Oh, who doesn't have money problems? Something will turn up.'

'Of course it will,' Liam agreed with her, and leaned across to refill her wineglass. 'You see the people who've just come in?' She could see them by pretending to be admiring the general décor, it meant swivelling round in her chair. 'Do you recognise the girl in the blue dress?'

The dress was baby-blue, cut very low. The girl had a cloud of pale fair hair and the face of an angel child. She was in a party of four whose general appearance screamed show-biz, and Carly blinked, 'No, but I'm sure I should,' and when Liam named a film star, none of whose films she had seen but whose name everybody knew, she whistled soundlessly and joked, 'Should I be asking for her autograph?'

'I shouldn't bother,' said Liam. 'She's so thick, she probably can't write.'

'Who'd need to, looking like that? I didn't realise we were eating with celebrities.'

'A few,' he said. They had a lovely seat for seeing without being seen. Not that anyone would recognise Carly, but Liam might be known, and this alcove provided cover as he identified other diners for her. He kept her giggling, telling scandalous tales about their love lives.

'I don't know how they find the energy,' she gurgled. 'It must get *so* complicated.'

'Not if you keep an appointments diary.'

'You're speaking from experience? That's what you do?' She was fooling, it was all bubbling and bright, and he smiled with her.

'Sometimes,' he said. 'Some of them have been forgettable. How about you? How many lovers do you have?'

She talked. Why not? None of it had been serious. She asked, when she was up to date and had explained how Barney was finding it hard to believe she didn't want to share his apartment, 'Is Victoria forgettable?

Do you remember time and place when you're meeting her?'

'She reminds me,' Liam shrugged.

'I'll bet,' said Carly. She could see Victoria Hayden on the phone making sure that Liam turned up for their date. She could remember her fingers clutching his arm at the birthday party.

'By the way,' he said gently, 'did you ever hear what happened to Gerald Collett when he came out of prison?'

Carly was eating a cassis sorbet and it was as though she bit on a piece of jagged ice in the melting smoothness. 'No,' she said.

'Of course not,' said Liam.

'Did you?'

'No.' There was silence for a few seconds. There had been silences before, of course, but this one seemed different to Carly. Gerald's name had shattered her peace of mind. She did know that he only served half the sentence, with remission for good behaviour, because for a while she had kept in touch with friends in the town where she had known him. 'It was an evil day when I met you,' he had written in the letter his father had handed her outside the court. 'And now for God's sake keep away from me.' She had done Gerald no deliberate harm, but he had tried to brand her, and at the very least it was tactless of Liam to question her about him.

Tactless and a little cruel, unless it had some real purpose. Carly couldn't think what, and when she looked up from the purple sorbet she was stirring in her dish Liam said, 'You must try that some time with vodka poured over it. It's a pleasant combination.'

'Lethal, I should think,' she commented, and everything went on as before, the meal drawing to an end with coffee for both and brandy for him. 'Not for me,' she said. 'It was a lovely wine and a delicious meal.' She was still smiling, but strangely sober as though a warning bell had struck. Liam had told her he had rung the Château, while he was waiting for her to come down, and spoken to Roland and Madame Corbé. They sent her their regards. Now as she drained her coffee cup she said, 'I'd like to have spoken to your aunt and Roland. Is it too late to say goodnight?'

It was late. It was probably silly, but she no longer trusted Liam completely and a word with Madame Corbé or Roland would have been reassuring. Liam was looking doubtful, telling her 'My aunt will certainly be in bed. I suppose we could get Roland, although there doesn't seem much point.'

'No,' she agreed. 'Well, I think I'll call it a day,' and now those rooms with the connecting door had begun to worry her. Liam mentioning Gerald meant he still had reservations about her, and doors would stay locked tonight because she now had reservations too.

'Don't you hurry,' she told him. There was still brandy in his glass. But he was on his feet, close behind her. She started to say how tired she was when someone shrieked, '*Liam!*' and it was the angel-faced girl in the baby-blue dress, with which the other three at her table all sat up and took notice and obviously Liam would have to go across to them, and say goodnight.

'Goodnight, then,' said Carly, and kept on walking, quickening her pace slightly until she was out of the dining room. She went straight upstairs to her room, she hadn't bothered about the bolt on the connecting doors before. Then she picked up the phone by the bed and asked, 'Parlez-vous anglais?' when it was answered.

They did. 'I want to phone Madame Corbé, the Château des Sables, Guirec Vert' she said. 'Mr Sherrard phoned there once tonight, I think. He's in the dining room, he can give you the number.'

No trouble at all. They had the number, and as she waited Carly knew this wasn't necessary. Tomorrow she would be at the Château. She didn't seriously imagine that Liam had kidnapped her. Why should he? Unless he was Gerald's friend and something dreadful had happened to Gerald, and that wasn't likely, she would have heard about that somehow.

She was behaving idiotically. If she had been kidnapped they wouldn't be in a super hotel where everybody recognised him. Kidnapped? She had to be muzzy in the head to keep harping back to that. But that was the trouble, she was muzzy, her head was spinning, and it was all because Liam had asked her about Gerald. Until then she had been having a wonderful time, feeling secure and happy, but that had been like a stone thrown straight at her face.

A man answered and she asked for Roland, then it was Roland and she said, 'Carly here.'

'Hello!' He sounded pleased. 'I'm glad you rang, I was wondering whether to give you a call.'

'You know where I am?' Of course he knew where she was. 'Liam rang,' he explained, and of course Liam had rung. Carly said, 'It's a fantastic place.'

'Isn't it?'

'We've just had a wonderful meal.'

'You would have,' said Roland. 'I suppose it was a good idea to break the journey, although I had hoped you'd be here tonight.'

She sat down on the bed, relaxing a little. 'So had I, I thought I'd be seeing you today. I was very surprised when Liam turned up at the airport.'

'He was coming over and he managed to get a seat on your flight.' That was how Liam had explained it, and perhaps she was over-sensitive about Gerald Collett. Perhaps that had just been a casual question, meaning nothing in particular. 'Is he with you?' Roland was asking.

'I left him downstairs, he met someone he knew— Alison Parry,' and Roland chuckled,

'She was a girl-friend of his, for a few weeks.'

'He said she was thick,' Carly muttered. Alison Parry had looked delighted when she spotted him, so perhaps the reunion would go on, perhaps he would stay with her tonight.

'How are you two getting on?' Roland enquired, and she said, 'All right.'

'Good.' He chuckled again. 'But don't get too confidential with him. Remember not to say anything that could be used in evidence.'

She said lightly, 'He's a lawyer, isn't he, not a policeman?'

'Ever seen him in court?' She knew that Roland was smiling, but the time she had seen Liam in court filled her mind, in harsh clear detail. She could see him now, looking down on her from that gallery. 'I mean in action,' added Roland.

He had been quite still, grim as granite. Roland meant had she ever watched Liam conducting a case, and he knew she hadn't or she would have mentioned it before. 'No,' she said. 'Why?'

'Nobody's better at lulling the victim into dropping their guards,' said Roland, 'and then—pow! He's a cold-blooded bastard, although I love him like a brother.'

Carly tried to laugh. He was, half seriously, putting her off Liam, he didn't want them getting too friendly, but he could be explaining everything that had happened since Liam took her arm in Birmingham airport and led her away from Barney. She looked at the connecting door and thought, you have no idea how close I was to being left with no defences at all. I could have slept with Liam tonight. She said, 'I just wanted to say goodnight.'

'Goodnight, my darling,' said Roland. 'See you tomorrow and don't let him persuade you to stop anywhere else on the way.'

'I won't, I promise you.' She put the phone down very gently as though it was fragile and might break, then sat very still. Liam hadn't told her that Alison Parry was an old brief flame. He had hardly told her anything about himself. It had all been about other people. They hadn't been swapping confidences, sharing secrets, although she had been chattering all manner of personal things. Of course, of *course*, she had been in the witness stand ever since he had lulled her into that sense of false security, into believing they were kindred spirits, into *wanting* him.

That was the bitter part. She would have opened that door tonight. She had been so near to falling badly for Liam, and that would have been dreadful.

She could be wrong. Roland could be wrong too. This time Liam might be acting without any ulterior motive, but, belatedly, all her instincts were telling her that he had flown out from England with her, and booked in here overnight, to learn all he could about her. Maybe seduction was part of the plan too. Things had certainly been heading that way until he had questioned her about Gerald. He had been too much the lawyer there, that had been his one mistake, showing how his mind was working.

If they had spent the night together it would probably have finished her with Roland. It would have labelled her easy, and that would have been ironic, because she was a million miles from promiscuous.

She got up, feeling stiff with tiredness, her fingers fumbling with the catch of her necklet. When it fell from her neck she flexed her muscles, which seemed to be in tight knots at the base of her skull. All the time she was undressing she couldn't keep her eyes from the connecting door, because she was pretty sure that Liam would tap on it sooner or later. Unless he went off with his old flame, unless he stayed talking and drinking with the party until it was too late to tap on any other woman's door.

If he hadn't been waylaid leaving the dining room they would have come upstairs together, and when they reached her room she would have said, 'Goodnight, I'll see you in the morning,' showing by voice and expression that she meant it, because things had changed for her even before she phoned Roland. She intended being friendly in the morning but nothing more. She had played far enough into Liam Sherrard's hands. Too far really, she wished now that she had told him less. But at least she had come to her senses before going completely overboard and literally into his hands.

She pulled the shining bronze dress over her head and the silken underskirt stroked her skin like cool fingertips, then she dragged it off and tossed it on to a chair. If he tapped on the door she wouldn't answer; she could have fallen asleep right away. She turned off the bedroom light, which might show under the door, finished removing her make-up in the bathroom, then climbed in between the sheets and expected to sleep because it had been a long day.

But she tossed for a long time, and when she tried to think pleasant thoughts—such as seeing Madame Corbé soon, and Roland, and the Château—it was always Liam's face that she saw. He couldn't have seemed closer if he had been standing by her bed. When she did sleep she dreamed fragments of the day: walking hand in hand through the market, sitting outside the café, the picnic lunch by the roadside, but it was all different. Darker, no sunshine, just a lot of shadows, and Liam looking at her with slitted eyes. He kept asking her very quietly, 'What happened to Gerald? Where is Gerald?' and at last she woke with a jerk and lay limp, and as exhausted as though she hadn't slept at all.

She was not responsible for Gerald Collett. He had never wanted to see her again and goodness knows she never wanted to see him, but she began to wonder whether there was anyone she could phone or write to, to find out if he had got his life together afterwards. Perhaps it was her fault. Gerald's counsel thought so, although Carly's friends had pointed out that it was his job to say anything that might lift some of the blame from his client.

She heard a tapping and shot up in bed, almost sure she had heard it before, that the sound not the dream had woken her. What was Liam playing at? He must think he was so fantastic if he expected her to open the door and go straight into his arms. She didn't stop to reflect that earlier she had been willing to do that. She was as indignant as though a stranger was accosting her, and she sat there, glaring in the direction of the door, considering getting out of bed and asking, 'What do you want?' and when he told her saying, 'You must be joking!'

Then the tapping came again, from the window. A wind had risen, and the window had blown loose from its catch, banging softly to and fro. Carly got up and closed it. Except for the keening of the wind everything was quiet, and after the warm bed the night air made her shiver.

It was dark outside. The stars that had seemed so bright when they came to the inn were hidden now by the clouds, and it was dark in the room. Carly felt her way back to bed, checking the time on the luminous face of her small travelling clock. It was nearly two, and she was wide awake now and relieved of course that there had been no scene with Liam. She wondered if he was in his room, and a wave of loneliness swept over her as bad as anything she had known for years.

She felt impatient with herself, and surprised because it took a lot to depress her and there was no reason for this. But as she huddled down in the darkness she could have turned her face into the pillow and sobbed herself sick.

But she didn't weep, and after a while she slept again, and when she woke for the second time the window pane was bright with sunshine, and again there was tapping. It was on the door to the corridor, and she pulled on her dressing gown and was greeted by the waitress of the previous night, who was carrying a tray. 'Good morning, *madame*.'

'Oh, good morning,' muttered Carly. 'Thank you.' She stood aside and the tray was deposited on a side table, and the waitress told her it was a beautiful day. Carly could see that for herself, but she smiled and agreed, and felt better after half a cup of coffee.

Although her reflection in the dressing table mirror looked heavy-eyed she went into the bathroom and splashed her face with cold water, then came back, still yawning, to spread the soft warm croissants with butter and strawberry preserve.

When she was packed and ready to leave she came out into the corridor and hesitated by Liam's door, then shrugged and kept on walking, down the stairs into the entrance hall, where Madame Louise was already at the desk and the telephone taking bookings. She looked round with a smile for Carly and said, 'Monsieur Sherrard is in the kitchens.'

'I'm going out for a breath of air,' said Carly. She had slept badly and there was an exhausting drive ahead, but the morning air was fresh. There were still several cars in the car park, one with a British registration number that could belong to the show-biz party, but nobody was about and Carly went across to the archway in the wall where she thought the rose garden ought to be.

There was a garden, but it was entirely devoted to vegetables, not a rose in sight nor a hint of fragrance in the air, and she stood frowning. She *had* smelled roses last night. Perhaps the woman walking ahead of them into the inn had worn a floral perfume, or maybe she had imagined the smell of roses. There had been a kind of magic about yesterday, almost like falling in love, and Carly tried to laugh at herself for such a crazy notion. But the smile was twisted, and as she walked down the straight paths between the rows of growing vegetables it turned into a heartfelt sigh.

'Carly!' Liam hailed her. She was at the far end of the vegetable garden by then, he had just come through the archway. 'Ready for off?' he asked, and she called back,

'Quite ready.'

The sun glinted on his dark hair. He didn't come to meet her, and she retraced her steps slowly because although she wanted to be on their way she was reluctant to go to him. She felt that getting too close might be a risky business. Like the spider and the fly, she thought, and reaching him she said, 'I rang the Château last night.'

'Did you?'

'I got Roland, who warned me not to get too confidential with you. He said you were a great one for worming out secrets.'

'What nonsense,' said Liam smoothly, and they walked towards the car side by side, and he opened the passenger door. 'I'll fetch your case,' he said.

'Have we settled the bill?'

'Yes.'

'I'd like to pay my share.'

'I couldn't hear of it.' He had gone before Carly could say,

'Oh yes, you could, you're hearing it now. How much?' Today she was determined to owe him nothing. He might be genuinely friendly, or he could be out to trap her in some way. She didn't know which, but this morning she was on her guard.

When he came out of the hotel Alison Parry was with him. She was wearing a cream silk suit, nearly the colour of her hair, and laughing at something Liam was saying. Illogically Carly felt she was the joke, and as they came together towards the car she began to smile herself, a cool superior smile, so that when they reached her she was ready for them. 'You haven't met

Alison, have you?' said Liam, and Carly drawled, 'Hello,' and thought, I'm probably as good an actress as you when it comes to the pinch.

Close up Alison Parry was breathtaking, and she had a husky sexy voice although she was only saying, 'Hello,' back, then ignoring Carly altogether. 'Now you *will* phone me real soon?' she said to Liam. 'You promise?'

'Of course,' said Liam, getting into the car. 'And good luck with the film.'

Alison Parry waved as the car drew away and Carly said tartly, 'Victoria would have found that fascinating. Old friend, is she?'

'Twenty-eight last month,' said Liam.

'Youngish friend, then. Gorgeous, but thick, I think you said. You don't go in for high IQ females, do you?'

'What makes you think that?'

It was another beautiful day. The sun was shining again, the sun roof was open, but the carefree camaraderie had gone. Now there was an edge to their talk. 'You're the one who said Alison Parry was thick,' said Carly, 'and I don't know much about Victoria, but if I'd listened to her with my eyes shut I'd have thought she was a pre-teenager.' That breathy little-girl voice had sounded childish, and Liam grinned.

'Oh, Victoria's bright enough.'

'Bright enough for what?' muttered Carly, and resolved to say no more about his lady friends because she was being surprisingly bitchy, and none of them were any of her business. Except that she had talked about the men in her life last night while he hadn't said a word about his own affairs.

She settled back in her seat and the miles slid by,

along roads which were straight avenues of poplars between unfenced, unhedged fields stretching away into the distance. In the fields she caught occasional glimpses of giant horses pulling ploughs, and every so often Liam slowed down to enter a village, or a small market town, where the buildings were festooned with climbing plants, and window boxes made splashes of colour against the yellow and red and green shutters.

They stopped for lunch at a small hotel in one town, and Carly was careful what she was telling him when they talked. The conversation was more like that of polite strangers and they didn't linger over this meal. Liam appeared as anxious to reach the Château as she was, the pleasure of her company was obviously palling.

Driving along after lunch they hardly talked at all. Carly had taken the map out of the glove compartment earlier, and been following the route on it all along, so she didn't have to ask where they were, and she couldn't think of anything else to say. Although with almost anyone else she would have been chattering.

The coastline was like Cornwall, on a grander scale. For miles there were stark rocky promontories, craggy out-thrusts into a breaking sea, with stretches of smooth golden sands between. From the coast road tracks led off to tiny fishing villages and here and there to a holiday complex of chalets and caravans, while on the higher crags old blockhouses and gun-sites and what looked like castle ruins reared against the skyline; and when the coast road swept low they could see the waves breaking with a roar and sometimes the wind tossed spray over the windscreen.

Carly was biting her lip to stop herself exclaiming, 'Look at this!' or asking, 'What's over there?' but she

was determined not to behave like a tourist in front of
Liam, so she kept her excitement to herself, presenting
him—if he should glance her way—with a slightly
bored profile.

Until the road sign said Guirec Vert, and then she
forgot about acting blasé and leaned forward eagerly.
When the car turned off the road, through a gateway
with two stone beasts rearing up either side, she swi-
velled in her seat to look back at them, asking, 'What
are they?'

'Lions rampant. The winged variety.'

'That's handy, if they should want to fly.'

'It's reckoned to be a thousand years since the last
time,' he said, 'but you don't need to worry.'

That must be a local legend, that she would hear
later. She wasn't asking Liam about it. Besides, she
was speechless for the moment; Madame Corbé's home
was a very impressive sight.

The drive was flanked by full-grown poplar trees,
leading to the wide semi-circular sweep of steps before
the main door. Either side of the broad steps were great
stone jars, perforated on the sides and vivid with
geraniums. The house had probably been red brick
once but mellowed almost to yellow, with a mass of
ivy covering one side. Attic windows pierced the steep
slope of the slated roof and a dozen or so twisted brick
chimneys rose against the skyline. The western wing
swept almost to the cliff edge, backed by a tall tower
that must give a fantastic view over the sea.

It was an old old house. The stories it could tell,
thought Carly, staring up as Liam parked near the
flight of steps. She could feel his eyes on her, but she
couldn't look at him, then the great door opened and
Roland came hurrying down the steps, and then she

Now...bring twice
as much romance
into your life
with a home
subscription to
SUPERROMANCES™

Yours
FREE.
Love beyond Desire

A compelling love story of mystery and intrigue... conflicts and jealousies... and a forbidden love that threatens to shatter the lives of all involved with the aristocratic Lopez family.

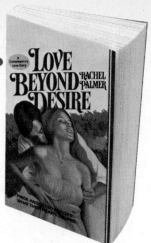

Now...you can bring romance into your life, every month, with a subscription to **SUPERROMANCES**, the almost 400 page romantic novels. Every month, three contemporary novels of romance will be in your mailbox. Twice as thick. Twice as much love.

SUPERROMANCES...begin with your **free** *Love beyond Desire.* Then month by month, look forward to three powerful love stories that will involve you in spellbinding intrigue.

SUPERROMANCES...exciting contemporary novels, written by the top romance novelists of today. And this huge value...each novel, almost 400 pages... is yours for only $2.50 a book. Hours of entertainment for so little. Far less than a first-run movie or pay-TV. Newly published novels, with beautifully illustrated covers, filled with pages of escape into a world of romantic love...delivered right to your home.

Bring twice as much romance into your life, beginning today. And receive *Love beyond Desire*, **free.** It's yours to keep even if you don't buy any additional books. Mail the postage-paid card below.

SUPER?OMANCE
1440 South Priest Drive, Tempe, AZ 85281.

↙ Mail this card today for your FREE book.

A compelling love story of mystery and intrigue... conflicts and jealousies... and a forbidden love that threatens to shatter the lives of all involved with the aristocratic Lopez family.

←—Mail this card today for your **FREE** book.

moved, scrambling out of the car.

She was very pleased to see Roland. He gave her a welcoming hug and kiss, and she smiled, 'Oh, it's lovely to be here!'

Liam was still watching her. He got out of the car too, he was standing beside them, and his expression was cynical, as though someone was telling him something he didn't believe. Carly had looked into his face when Barney was kissing her goodbye, and she wondered why this man could make her feel so insecure even when she had arms around her, and someone who was fond of her holding her close. Now she was experiencing that feeling again and she almost ran up the steps to where Madame Corbé was standing in the doorway. Roland was nice, Carly was pleased to see him again, but she had a real tenderness for the upright old lady who had been so anxious that Carly should visit her home.

Madame Corbé held out her arms and Carly thought, maybe I am looking for a grandmother. Maybe she wished she was Antoinette, coming home, and she must guard against that dangerous daydream.

Madame Corbé kissed Carly. 'It is good you're both here, safe and sound. Liam looked after you?'

'Very well,' said Carly.

'Not too well, I hope,' said Roland, smiling. 'Although I hear you met Alison Parry at Les Deux Soeurs.' Madame Corbé looked enquiringly and Roland explained, 'His birds turn up everywhere,' and the old lady shook her head with tolerant affection.

'It was very convenient that Liam managed to get away for a few days,' she said. 'That you could travel together.'

'Extremely convenient,' drawled Liam, and his eyes

glinted as he smiled at Carly and she thanked her stars
that she hadn't spent the night with him. That would
have given him a trump card to play against her, because she was no longer fooling herself that they were
anything but bitter opponents.

'You'll want to go to your room,' said Madame
Corbé, and Carly said, 'Yes, please.'

A woman who had been hovering in the background
stepped forward, and Liam asked, 'Which room?'

'The room by the schoolroom,' said Madame Corbé,
and Liam said,

'I think another would be preferable.'

They must be referring to Antoinette's room and
Carly wondered how she could ask for somewhere else,
but while she hesitated Madame Corbé put a hand on
Liam's arm and said, 'It has been a guest room for a
long time.'

'I suppose it has,' he conceded grudgingly, and the
woman who had picked up Carly's case went off with
it towards the staircase.

Carly was relieved to find the room uncluttered. She
has been apprehensive that it might have been left as it
was when Antoinette slept here. Books around, perhaps, a doll on the bed, even a child's clothes in the
cupboards. But she could see no intimate personal
things, and after the middle-aged woman in the dark
dress smiled and nodded and left, she hung up some of
her clothes.

It was an attractive room, thick-carpeted in a warm
honey shade, the furniture white and gold—not speci-
fically a child's room. Antoinette could have grown up
in here. If she had she would have been Roland's age
now, and Carly shivered slightly. 'Someone walking
over my grave,' she thought, and went to the window

to clear her mind of depressing and pointless brooding.

The window had a sea view and she stood for a few minutes drinking in the loneliness and the beauty, particularly intrigued by a shape like broken towers rising far out. She would ask about them when she went downstairs. She must remember all about everything in this fabulous place to tell Ruth and William. William would like the winged lions at the gate. She could make up some bedtime stories for him about them.

There was a bathroom, in which she freshened up, then she sat down at the dressing table retouching her make-up and brushing her hair. She might get used in a little while to looking into Antoinette's mirror, but she really would have preferred another room.

She was wondering now whether she had been wise to come, and she brushed her hair slowly, thoughtfully, eyes downcast.

There were porcelain pots and tray on the dressing table, and a little matching box, ivory porcelain dotted with tiny flowers, and she put down her hairbrush and lifted the lid, admiring the exquisite detail of a pink rosebud.

Inside the box was a fine silver chain with blue stones at intervals. Perhaps it had been Antoinette's, it was the kind of thing a young girl might wear, and Carly took it out, feeling sadness. It was so fragile and so pretty. Poor child, she thought, and for no particular reason held the chain round her own throat, looking at herself in the mirror, and the fastener clicked between her fingers.

She couldn't go down wearing this. Whoever it belonged to it didn't belong to her. As she fumbled, trying to undo it, someone rapped on the door and she called, 'Come in.' When Liam opened the door she automatically covered her throat with her hands. 'They're waiting for you,' he told her.

'I'm coming.'

'Then come,' he said. He stood, inside the doorway, waiting, and Carly had to drop her hands before she could start on the clasp again and he snarled, 'And you can take that off for a start!'

'I'm trying to take it off.'

His eyes were blazing. 'Why did you put it on?'

'I don't know. I opened this box and it was there. Was it——?'

'Antoinette's? Yes, it was, and don't think because you're in this room that you're taking over in any other way.'

'I didn't ask to be put in here,' she protested. 'Your aunt said it had been a guest room for a long time.'

'It has.' Liam was right beside her now, leaning over her, it seemed, and she swayed back on the stool. 'But you're the first guest in it.'

'D-don't they have many guests, then?'

'I've seen every other room full,' he said. 'But nobody in here. And get that necklace off!'

Carly's hands were shaking, he made her shake, he was too close. 'It's a tricky clasp,' she muttered, 'I can't seem——' and he reached for her, and she tried to slide under his hands.

She knew all he was going to do was undo the fastener, but she panicked as wildly as though she was about to be assaulted, and when his hand closed on her shoulder she hit out with both hands and he threw her back, farther and harder than he need have done, so that she spun half across the room and ended in a heap against the bed.

Liam said nothing and neither did she. They glared furiously at each other, then he said, 'Don't come down wearing it,' and his voice sounded strangled, and he went out of the room while Carly got to her knees, and her jaw fell open.

It was crazy. They were fighting—physically. She had tried to claw him and he had thrown her across the room. She had started it, but he hadn't asked what the hell she thought she was doing. He hadn't even seemed surprised. He had just fought back, chucking her out of the way.

It's crazy! she thought. I never met a man before who could bring on this howling red rage. She looked at her hands, as though they were a stranger's, then got to her feet and went back to the mirror and looked at herself.

I could kill him, she thought, but my gosh, I'd better not try it again, because he is more than capable of killing me!

CHAPTER FIVE

CARLY'S hands were shaking so badly that she could break the fastener of the necklet if she went on fumbling with it. She eased it round on her neck and peered into the mirror. The catch looked simple enough, just the slip-on type, but she couldn't pull it apart with a gentle tug and she daren't risk any kind of force.

She would have to ask somebody to take it off for her. Not Liam. Roland, as soon as she could get Roland on his own, because she didn't want Madame Corbé seeing it. It wasn't all that unusual, although if the blue stones were sapphires it could be valuable. But Liam had recognised it at once as Antoinette's and it might distress Madame Corbé, seeing another girl wearing it.

By tying a scarf around her throat she managed to hide it, and after a few deep breaths felt composed enough to go downstairs and face them all.

There was no sign of Liam when she came out of her room, and she stood for a moment, getting her bearings. This house was big enough to lose yourself in. And quiet. She passed closed doors and wondered which had been the schoolroom, which perhaps led to the tower, remembering a painting, a piece of sculpture, and finally reaching the staircase.

Liam looked cool enough when she walked into the room, following the sound of voices. Madame Corbé and Roland turned smiling faces on her, Liam looked at her, straight and unsmiling, as though nothing in the world would make him lose control. Yet less than five minutes ago he had used force against her.

He knew she was still wearing the necklet. His eyes were on the green silk scarf, folded choker fashion, and Carly gulped, feeling that the scarf was too tight, wanting to loosen it.

A meal was waiting. They ate in a little dining room, and drank a cold white wine and discussed plans for Carly's holiday. Roland reminded her of his promise to teach her riding, and she laughed and said she wasn't so sure about that, horses always seemed so big close to. The only riding she had done was on a donkey at the village fête when the donkey stopped dead and sent her over its head on to the tombola stall.

She added gravely while they were laughing, 'That

was when I decided I wasn't a natural horsewoman.
The donkey stopped whenever he felt like it all through
the afternoon, but nobody else actually went over his
head!

Swimming? Roland suggested, and that was different, Carly was enthusiastic about that, but Madame
Corbé warned, 'You must take care. The rocks and the
currents here can be dangerous.'

'I'll keep you from the rocks,' said Roland cheerfully, and Carly thanked him and thought, I'll swim
with you, but not with Liam. Liam would have no
qualms about steering me into danger.

There were places she had to see: towns, beauty
spots, ruins; she asked, 'Are there some ruins out at
sea? I think I saw them from the bedroom window.'

'You walk out when the tide's out,' Roland told her.
'There was a chapel there in the twelfth century, built
by a Breton chief, giving thanks for his daughter's
miraculous escape.'

'Escape from what?' Carly asked. 'The plague?' She
had seen two stone carved calvaries on the road here,
and she knew those had been erected after the passing
of the Black Death.

'From being ravished by pirates,' said Roland, giving
it a ring of melodrama.

'Oh dear!' said Carly. 'Such goings on! And how did
she escape?'

'The story is,' said Madame Corbé with a twinkle in
her eye, 'that around 1100 a very beautiful and very
pious young lady was walking along the beach one
evening when a boat pulled in and some very fierce
men stepped out. The captain was about to force his
attentions on her when she called on the saints for pro-
tection.'

'Virgins were always doing that in those days,' Roland chimed in.

'And what did the saints do?'

'The stone lions at the gates of her father's house,' said Roland, 'sprouted wings and flew over and carried her back to safety while the pirates beat a fast retreat. And that's the legend of the winged lions of Guirec Vert.'

'Which are at your gate?' exclaimed Carly.

'Not the originals, I'm afraid,' Madame Corbé smiled. 'But perhaps they would follow tradition and protect us in time of trouble. I've always been very fond of them.'

'I'm sure they would,' said Carly. 'Can visitors call on them for help?'

'They've got a strict code of conduct,' Liam drawled. 'They only operate for the virtuous.' So that was what he'd meant when their car came through the gates and he had said no lions would be flying for her. Roland took it that Liam was joking, but Madame Corbé frowned disapprovingly, considering it bad taste for a gentleman to make such insinuations about a lady.

'And how would you know I don't qualify?' asked Carly, smiling sweetly.

'Oh, I feel I know you very well,' said Liam. He was sitting opposite her, smiling, but not with his eyes, and she said,

'You don't know me at all.' That wasn't true. He knew things she hadn't known herself until she met him. Until then she had never imagined that anyone could make her lose emotional control as easily as he could.

And it worked the other way round. She brought out the savage in him. If Madame Corbé considered his remark about Carly's morals were insulting what would she think if Carly said, 'Believe me, that's nothing. Just now we had a fight and he knocked me down.'

She wouldn't believe it. Neither would Roland. Nor do I, thought Carly, while we're sitting here and he's looking far too civilised to raise his hand to a woman. Any more than I would dream of hitting out at a man who was only offering to undo the clasp of a necklet.

It was the eyes that gave him away, but only to her, it seemed. When she looked straight into his eyes, into the dark centre, she got a little shock like the brush of a live wire. She wondered if he saw it in her eyes too, whatever it was that nobody else noticed, and she turned to Madame Corbé and began to talk, fast.

'I love legends. I've heard of flying dragons, but not flying lions before. William will love it—Ruth's little boy, he's always on the lookout for a new bedtime story. Of course I'll have to make her a princess. Nothing less will do for William. By the way, she wasn't an ancestress of the Corbés, was she?'

A thousand years was a long time, but some families could trace their family tree that far, but Madame Corbé told her, 'My husband came from Paris before I was married. I was born here. My name was Cherreur' ... Sherrard, the anglicised version ... 'And we arrived here in the seventeenth century, long after the miracle of the flying lions.' She smiled, 'Which is of course only a story.'

'Oh *no*!' Carly protested. 'Wonderful things used to happen. There used to be dragons and knights in shining armour and witches and warlocks. And pirates, of course.' She was probably talking too much, Liam's expression was wry. 'I can see you as a pirate,' she said. 'I shouldn't be at all surprised if one of your ancestors was in that boat.'

'Can you?' he drawled. 'Well, I sure as hell can't see you as the virgin,' and Madame Corbé gasped, *'Liam!'* turning quite pale with shock.

'Sorry,' he said cheerfully, and grinned at her, and she said faintly,

'You young people say such things. That was not funny.'

He's not so young, thought Carly sourly, and he isn't trying to be funny. He's older in the head than you will ever be, dear Madame Corbé, and I notice he's only saying sorry to you. She smiled and said, 'Your apology is accepted,' and he could hardly point out that he wasn't apologising to her.

Later in the evening there was a caller. After the meal they went into the kind of drawing room Carly had only visited on the Stately Homes circuit. She felt there should have been a long strip of protective covering across the fabulous old carpet, and a roped-off barrier with little arrows pointing the Way Out. It seemed odd to march boldly across, skirting all the beautiful things, and sit down beside Madame Corbé on one of the brocaded settees, with her feet on a Persian rug.

Madame Corbé had brought out photograph albums and was showing Carly pictures of herself when she was a young woman, with her husband and the boy who would later be Antoinette's father. She was at the beginning of the first album. They were thick and there were three of them. Carly reckoned that Liam and Roland and Antoinette would probably be making their first appearances in the second. A record of growing up. Not Antoinette, her span was tragically brief. But she would see how the years had changed the two men who sat some distance away, talking over what looked like business papers.

Carly found the photographs fascinating. Old pictures always were, especially when you could recognise somebody in them, and Madame Corbé was exactly as Carly had imagined her, quite beautiful. But more than once she caught herself sneaking a look across at Liam and Roland.

Liam sat with the papers before him, while Roland sat in a listening attitude most of the time, leaning forward, nodding, taking in what Liam was saying. They weren't discussing her. She could have heard them, if she had concentrated on hearing; but when she did for a moment it was something about strawberries. Her name wasn't mentioned, that would have reached her through Madame Corbé's soft-spoken reminiscences.

The caller was a short stocky man, with thinning grey hair and a broad jovial face. He came into the room like someone sure of a welcome, and his greeting was echoed by them all. He went straight to Madame Corbé: '*Madame*. . . .'

'*Mon cher* Louis!'

'*Vous allez bien ce soir?*'

'*Oui, très bien.*'

'*Bon, bon.*' He was holding her hand and, Carly noticed, checking her pulse. So he was a doctor, and this seemed like a regular occurrence and if it was necessary Madame Corbé must be ailing.

That frightened Carly, as though they had been close for a long time. But Madame Corbé was getting old and perhaps he was simply checking as a precaution. Madame Corbé was introducing her to Dr Castel, then Carly's hand was ceremoniously kissed and she was asked in fluent English what part of England she came from.

The doctor knew Carly's area, he said, he and his daughter had been guests at Liam's home, and Carly imagined a woman looking like the doctor. She wouldn't be Liam's type. She could be well over forty, going by her father, so they must be family friends.

It would be good to have friendships that lasted a long time, books of photographs that showed you with everybody who had loved you. She wished passionately that she was in those dark-blue velvet-covered albums, and this was her home, her family. She wished she had been Antoinette, with a right to Madame Corbé's love, and Roland for her brother, and Liam not hating her.

'You will have a glass of wine, of course,' said Madame Corbé, and Roland was pouring and they all sat together, and Carly knew she was daydreaming, but nobody else knew she was pretending that she belonged.

She sat back, in the deep soft cushions, and listened. They spoke in English; it would probably have been French if she hadn't been there. 'We were very impressed at the way you handled that criminal libel case last month,' said the doctor to Liam. 'Your cross-examination was masterly.' He rolled his eyes. 'Such damages!'

'Gratifying, but a little excessive, I thought,' said Liam, and Carly found herself grimacing. She could visualise Liam as a prosecutor only too easily.

Roland grinned across at her, 'They don't call him the Inquisitor for nothing! Never been known to lose his nerve yet.'

'Do they call you the Inquisitor?' she asked.

'Of course not,' said Liam.

'But you've never been known to lose your nerve?'

'Not in court,' he said, and a moment later a phone rang and a man came in to say that Monsieur Liam was wanted.

'We told you Victoria phoned last night,' said Roger. 'She expected you to ring her as soon as you got here, so what are you going to tell her?'

'Not a lot,' said Liam.

'I'd say Victoria's on the way out,' said Roger, when Liam had closed the door, and asked Carly, 'Was Alison Parry as glamorous as she was last year?'

So Alison Parry was last year's girl, who wouldn't mind being this year's too. 'I'd never seen her before yesterday, but she's pretty fantastic,' said Carly.

The doctor and Madame Corbé were exchanging amused glances. 'That one,' said the doctor, 'is not looking for a wife.'

'Old friend,' said Madame Corbé, 'regrettably, you are right,' and she reached over and patted Roland's hand, her meaning obvious. Roland raised eyebrows, and smiling shook his head at her. She meant that her hopes for future generations rested with him, and Carly began to wonder if they might include her.

Oh no! she thought. Thank you, but no. And then she thought, This is rank conceit. She likes me, so does he like me, but nobody is going to hand-pick me to carry on this kind of dynasty.

The doctor stayed for about half an hour, and when he stood up to leave he asked Madame Corbé, '*Est-ce que vous avez assez de pilules?*' '*Oui, merci,*' she said.

Pilules? Pills? They could be sleeping pills, vitamins. But when the doctor had gone Carly asked quietly, 'What are you taking pills for?'

Madame Corbé made a gesture of disparagement,

'Oh, a little heart condition, nothing to worry about.'

But Carly would worry. She was concerned now, looking for signs of stress, although it was only at their first meeting that Madame Corbé had seemed tired and strained. She wanted to ask more questions, but that would have been tactless, and she bit her lip and momentarily forgot why she was wearing the scarf and eased it round a little, and Madame Corbé's eyes widened.

Liam swore, at least Carly thought he did. Madame Corbé didn't seem to hear him, she went on looking at Carly's throat, and Carly said, 'I—found it in the little box on the dressing table, and tried it on, and the fastener stuck. I was going to ask someone to undo it.' She looked helplessly at Roland, and Liam said,

'I offered to take it off for you.'

'I thought I could do it myself then.' She wouldn't have had this happen for the world. She didn't want Madame Corbé distressed in any way, and she said, 'I'm sorry, I'd no right to put it on. I just held it round my neck and the fastener clicked.'

'It looks very pretty on you, my dear.' Madame Corbé was smiling again. 'You must keep it.'

'Oh, I couldn't,' Carly protested, but Liam's 'No,' drowned her cry. 'Please,' she appealed to Roland, 'could you unfasten it?'

It took a few seconds. The clasp was either stiff or complicated, and she sat still, feeling Roland's fingers at the back of her neck, but a hundred times more conscious of Liam, who wasn't touching her at all.

When the silver chain slid loose she caught it and Liam held out his hand. She dropped it in his palm, not touching him, and he put the chain in his pocket. He was remembering how it had looked on Antoinette, so was Madame Corbé, of course, and Liam was blaming Carly for that. He might even think she had done it deliberately, that she wanted to remind Madame Corbé of her granddaughter. He certainly resented any suggestion that Carly should keep the chain, the way he had spoken up he wouldn't even have heard her refusal.

'I think,' said Madame Corbé, 'that I shall take my little walk now before I go to my room. Perhaps you would like to come with me?'

'Oh yes!' Carly scrambled to her feet. Madame Corbé didn't need helping up, but she took Carly's hand, and Carly put an arm around her; she felt small and slight, as though her bones were as brittle as a bird's. Liam watched with a twisted smile and again Carly knew what he was thinking, and she hated him for believing she felt anything for Madame Corbé but deep disinterested affection.

Long windows opened on to a terrace running around the house. It was a warm night, and when Madame Corbé and Carly stepped out it seemed as mild out here as it had been indoors. The sound of the sea, soft and whispering, filled the air, and moonlight lit their way. 'I walk along here each night,' said Madame Corbé, 'when the weather permits. I find it composes the mind.'

Oh, it does, thought Carly. All this beautiful silence, the star-studded sky and the sea, were making her feel wonderfully calm. There was a stone seat at the foot of the tower and Madame Corbé sat down. 'When I was younger,' she said, 'I used to climb the tower and look out. That was like being in the sky, but best of all was the island of the chapel when the tide came in.'

The tide was out. Beneath the cliffs was the strip of

gleaming sand then the rocks, great boulders some of them. 'I used to take my troubles out there,' Madame Corbé told her, 'and walk around, with the seabirds for company. It was my favourite place when I was a girl.'

A little breeze touched them and Carly asked, 'Would you like your shawl?'

She had been wearing one earlier, it was lying on a chair. 'I'll fetch it,' said Carly without waiting for an answer, and hurried back towards the open windows of the drawing room. She heard Roland's voice as she approached, sounding shrill, demanding, 'What's it add up to, anyhow?' and she walked softly.

'I'll tell you what it adds up to,' said Liam. 'The shop isn't making much of a living, but she goes short of nothing she wants. The man seeing her off at the airport thought she was moving in with him until she got a better offer. Aunt Aimée, presumably, and possibly you. Well, Aunt Aimée might not see through her, but by God, you'd better. Remember, one bloke landed in jail providing the good life for her, and she never even bothered to check what happened to him after that. He could have hanged himself for all she cared.'

The horror in Roland's voice was in Carly too. She froze, as Roland croaked, 'He didn't, did he?'

'No, he didn't,' said Liam, and she tore into the room, the ice melted in a flame of fury.

'No, he didn't!' she echoed savagely. 'Somebody would have told me if he had, but how do you know what happened to him?'

'Do you care?' drawled Liam, and she grated,

'I never want to see him again, but I hope he's all right. What do you know about him?'

'That he's alive and well and running a moderately successful business in stripped pine,' said Liam.

'Well, I'm glad to hear it. You said you didn't know Gerald.'

'I don't. I checked up after you turned up.'

Loathing for him rose in her so that she could have heaved. 'Hoping he'd hanged himself? Hoping I should have something ghastly on my conscience?' She had carried enough guilt for something that was not her fault, and she said bitterly, 'Did anyone ever ask what he did to me?'

'What did he do to you?' Liam's voice was deceptively gentle, just as it must often be in court.

Took away trust, stripped her of pride—but Liam was too cynical to believe that, and she shrugged, 'Nothing you'd understand.' She picked up Madame Corbé's shawl and looked at Roland for the first time. He seemed struck dumb. 'Goodnight, gentlemen,' she said.

She walked back along the terrace with her head high, although nobody was watching. It would have been all the same to Liam if she had crawled away. When she reached the stone seat she put the shawl around Madame Corbé's shoulders, then sat down and asked, 'Has Liam said anything to you about Gerald Collett?'

'Who's Gerald Collett?' So he hadn't. But he would, and it was better that Carly should try to explain first. She gripped the carved arm of the stone seat and said, 'Someone I met years ago. He went to prison for stealing and he'd spent a lot of money on me. I thought it was his money, but it wasn't, and Liam knows about it.' She took a great gulp of air. 'And he thinks that now I'm out to swindle you, or

anybody else who's fool enough to trust me. He must
think I'm some kind of——'

Words failed her. Well, she knew the words for what
Liam thought she was, but she couldn't say them, and
to her dismay her throat closed, and her eyes misted
and tears were pouring down her cheeks, dripping off
her chin.

'It's all right.' Madame Corbé put her arms around
her, gathering her in as though she was a child, and
Carly blinked mopping her face with her hands, hic-
cuping, 'I'm s-sorry, I can't remember when I last did
that.'

'He was talking about this just now? He has upset
you, hasn't he?' Madame Corbé sounded as though she
was soothing a child with a grazed knee, and Carly
said,

'No, he hasn't upset me,' which was stupid when
the tears were still wet on her cheeks. 'But it isn't fair,'
she muttered, 'because I'm n-not what he thinks I
am.'

'Come along.' Madame Corbé got up, taking Carly's
hand.

'Where?' She couldn't go back in, and that was the
direction that Madame Corbé was tugging. 'I can't go
in just yet.'

'Of course you can.'

It was surprising how the little hand had developed
quite a grip. If I struggle with her, thought Carly,
feeling hysterical laughter threatening, I could jerk her
off her feet. But Madame Corbé continued to pull on
Carly's hand, and very unwillingly Carly walked with
her.

She must look such a sight, her mascara must have
run, and she had probably smudged her lipstick too.

But why should she care? Blow the pair of them! Perhaps they wouldn't be there. There were enough rooms in this place, perhaps they'd have taken themselves off.

But they were more or less where she had left them. Roland sitting upright in an armchair, Liam lounging in another. They must have heard the approaching footsteps, because they weren't talking. They were both looking at the long windows with the draped curtains through which Carly and Madame Corbé reappeared, and Carly thought, it's like a play with an audience of two. Her cheeks were flaming now, so hot that the tears should be drying rapidly, and her eyes were burning.

'Liam,' said Madame Corbé, in her soft sweet tones, 'what is this all about? Look what you've done to Carly!'

He was looking. Carly couldn't tell what he was thinking, his face was expressionless, but he was looking at her. 'What *I've* done?' he echoed.

'She's been telling me about that foolish young man,' Madame Corbé went on. 'But Carly wasn't his keeper. She was deceived by him. So why are you bringing back these unhappy memories for her?' The hand she put on Liam's arm trembled. 'It isn't like you, being unkind.'

Not to you, thought Carly. That's why he's so prejudiced against me, because he thinks he's protecting you. And maybe the money. He suspects I'm after Antoinette's share. He must be loaded himself, but he doesn't want that.

Liam smiled a slow smile. 'All right—it's past history. We'll take Carly's word that she's all heart.' He patted the old lady's hand on his arm and she looked relieved, apparently unaware of the mockery behind his words.

'And you are going to be friends?' she persisted.

'Why not?' shrugged Liam.

Carly could have given a dozen good reasons why not, but when Madame Corbé turned anxiously to her she said, 'That *will* be nice—and now if you don't mind I think I'd better go to my room.' She couldn't stay down here with her tear-streaked face, and it was getting late; Madame Corbé said,

'Of course—goodnight, my dear,' and kissed her gently, and Carly wondered if she was remembering Antoinette as her lips brushed Carly's flushed cheek.

She said, 'Goodnight,' and Roland's 'Goodnight,' startled her; she had almost forgotten he was there. She went quickly. She was across the hall and at the bottom of the stairs before she realised she was being followed.

Roland? she thought, and turned, and it was Liam. Her instincts were to run for it and lock her door, but she knew he would catch her before she reached her room, so she stopped where she was, looking at him stonily, and demanded, 'Well, friend?'

He said, 'I think you and I had better have a truce when Aunt Aimée's around.'

She shrugged, exaggeratedly casual. 'As the man said just now—why not?'

'She can do without emotional scenes. As you realised tonight, she had a heart condition.' Carly bit her lip, hearing him say that. There was a frown line cutting deep between his brows. 'I didn't expect you to go out there and produce floods of tears,' he added.

He was suggesting it was part of an act, to enlist Madame Corbé's sympathy, and she gave a choked shriek of laughter. 'Neither did I expect it, for heaven's sake! I'd be some actress, wouldn't I, if I could do that? Those floods of tears were a safety valve blowing. If I hadn't burst into tears I would probably have gone looking for a hatchet, then come back looking for you.'

'You'd have found me.' The eyes were hooded. 'So long as you're here I'm never going to be more than two paces behind.'

'What makes you think you can keep up with me?' she snapped, and pushed past him and ran up the stairs. The painting at the top of the stairs was a man in a dark jacket with a white frilled jabot, sitting at a desk with his hand on a book. There were family portraits all over the place. The man at the top of the stairs had a stranger's face but Liam's long strong fingers and beautifully manicured nails. He's everywhere, Carly thought, and looked back to where he was still standing at the foot of the wide stairs, then hurried off in the direction of her bedroom.

She was shedding no more tears in this house, she decided when she saw her clown-streaked eyes and feverish face in the dressing table mirror. The tears hadn't been anger so much as misery as memories of Gerald had flooded back.

'You *idiot!*' she chided herself. She was supposed to be relaxing and enjoying herself, swimming, sightseeing, learning to ride. That was what Roland had promised her, but after listening to Liam just now Roland might have had second thoughts about her. He didn't seem to have said anything while the drama was being played out. Except, 'Goodnight,' and if tomorrow went on like this it would be, 'Goodbye.'

Carly jerked herself up. She had been sitting at the dressing table with her head in her hands, and that

was idiotic, because she didn't have to stay here. There
had to be some way she could get out of Guirec Vert,
if it was only by winged dragon. She made herself grin
at that, as though it was quite a joke. But the grin
didn't last. She was sighing again in the bathroom, and
curled up in Antoinette's bed she wished she was back
home, with Ruth and William within call.

She hoped Ruth wasn't lying awake worrying. All
the money this family must have, yet Ruth was worried
sick because the lease was going up by a few hundred
measly pounds. If they were sapphires in that necklet
and I'd accepted it, thought Carly, I could have sold it
and put the money into Ruth's account.

Liam wouldn't have been surprised if she'd held on
to it. He thought she was a dedicated grabber, and that
made her so angry, so mad, she was thrashing around
as though she had a fever, until the quilt slithered off
and she had to lean over to retrieve it. After that she
tried to lie still, hugging the down-filled coverlet
around her and thinking how nice it would be to have
someone to snuggle up to.

'Come and share my home,' Barney had said, but
she wouldn't. It wasn't Barney whose comfort and
loving she needed.

Next morning she was determined, if there was any
tension in the atmosphere when she got downstairs,
she was staying no longer than it took to arrange her
journey home. If Liam's prejudices had rubbed off on
Roland she was off. She hadn't expected Liam to be
here. As he was, he was all the aggro she was taking.
But as she walked down the staircase Roland came
hurrying to meet her and enquire, 'Did you sleep well?'
Before she could answer he added, 'Of course you did,
or you wouldn't look so blooming.'

She hadn't slept well, but her make-up was skilfully applied, and she said wryly, 'Remembering how I looked last night it wouldn't be hard to look better.'

'About last night,' he shifted uncomfortably, 'I'm sorry you overheard what Liam was saying. There'd have been no scene at all if you hadn't.'

Carly raised her eyebrows. 'You mean if I hadn't heard him saying that Gerald could have hanged himself for all I cared you'd have told him to shut up?'

'Yes,' said Roland.

'I wouldn't have minded hearing that.' She was sure Roland would have listened as long as Liam had talked, but this was a friendly gesture, so she smiled,

'Oh, let's forget it.'

A broad beam spread over his face, and he took her hand as Liam came into the hall. 'Lovely day,' said Liam.

'It was,' said Carly.

'This morning,' said Liam, 'we're going to show you around.'

'Both of you?'

'Not necessarily,' said Liam, deliberately misunderstanding. 'I'm on holiday, but I expect Roland has work waiting.'

'Nothing that can't wait,' said Roland.

Carly had breakfasted in her room. Now she was taken round the Château. The sun shone through the old convex panes in the tall narrow windows, as she went from room to room, admiring, exclaiming. There was so much to see—the paintings by famous artists, French and English, the family portraits. The English branch dated from just after the first world war, and in every picture Carly caught herself looking for Liam, occasionally glimpsing some similarity, although it was usually Roland who told her the names, and if there was anything worth telling, what they had done.

There really was a bed in which Napoleon once slept in the summer of 1813. It was in an oak-panelled room, a black four-poster with saffron-yellow curtain drops and covers, and Carly asked, 'Does anyone ever sleep in here?'

'Occasionally,' said Liam. 'The only shrine in this house was Antoinette's room,' and Carly turned to Roland.

'I wish your aunt hadn't put me in there. I shouldn't be in Antoinette's place in any way.'

'We do know,' said Liam.

'I'd really like another room.'

'How about this?' suggested Liam.

Carly stroked the damask bed hangings. 'Is all this original?' It was, and that settled it. 'I'd never dare sleep in here! I'd be terrified of spilling coffee or tearing a sheet if I had a nightmare. But I'd love to tell them back home that I'd sat on Napoleon's bed.'

'Be our guest,' said Liam. She sat gingerly on the bed's edge and he knelt down, slipping off first one of her shoes, then the other, and her toes curled. 'Lie back, and think of Napoleon,' he ordered. He swung her feet on to the bed and her head went back. It wasn't the most comfortable of beds, it felt rather hard, but she stretched out luxuriously, smiling as Liam looked down at her.

Suddenly his dark mocking face became serious and a small muscle twitched in his cheek, and she almost cried out. Then Roland said something about the stone fireplace, and she got off the bed and put on her shoes, and pretended to examine the coat of arms carved above the fireplace: the flying lion, the latticed pattern, words on a scroll 'Resurgam—Guirec.'

If Roland hadn't been in the room she would have cried out Liam's name. But Liam was talking about the family of stonemasons who had carved the fireplace, their descendants still lived in Guirec Vert. His voice was so calm it sounded slightly bored; perhaps she had misread the desire that had seemed so nakedly apparent to her a moment ago.

Roland hadn't noticed. She could have been wrong. But she was almost sure that, looking at her lying there, Liam had wanted her fiercely, and that if he had moved to take her she could have gone up like tinder.

CHAPTER SIX

LIAM didn't like her, but physically he wanted her, and that would have been fine, and flattering, if she hadn't found him so disturbing. If she could stay cool the power would be hers.

Carly had never realised before that physical chemistry could exist without liking, but even now she was wondering what would have happened if Roland had not been in that bedroom, remembering Liam's suddenly urgent face and her answering surge of desire. She knew what would have happened, and as they walked along the corridor she began reminding herself why she disliked Liam.

Because he blamed her for Gerald, and that was so unfair. Because he was cold as a cobra beneath the charm. Keep that well in mind, she told herself, and

don't ever let him get you alone. Don't even let him
brush against you, because contact is dynamite.

The schoolroom was next to Antoinette's room. It
could have been still in use, with the pupils on holiday.
There was no dust on the big mahogany table that
filled the centre of the room. The wall blackboard was
wiped clean, but there were chalks in the ledge beneath, and a smaller table at which a tutor must have
sat. Cupboards were closed, and Carly wondered if
textbooks were still stacked inside. Exercise books too,
perhaps, with a round childish script.

She asked, 'Were you——?' and she could almost
see them, the three of them.

'No,' said Roland. 'We were at boarding school in
England. Liam went on to Cambridge and I came here
afterwards. The schoolroom was always like this in the
holidays, but in here we had some happy hours.'

A big playroom led off the schoolroom, with cupboards again, and toys around. A dolls' house, a great
rocking horse with flaring nostrils and silky black mane
and tail. Carly said impulsively, 'These must be worth
a fortune. But you don't need the money, do you? It
must be lovely to be able to keep them.'

She opened the front of the dolls' house, going down
on her knees and peering with wonder at the minute
world in there. Such perfect tiny pieces, furniture as
beautiful as the furniture of the Château. And dolls in
old-fashioned clothes, no bigger than her fingers, looking up at her with tiny white faces.

Antoinette must have played with them. Perhaps she
had set them for the last time in their chairs, leaning
against a table, sitting at a piano. And the baby in a
crib in the nursery with a kitten curled up on a rug the
size of a postage stamp.

Carly closed the door gently. The rocking horse could easily be a hundred years old, and the dolls' house. It was a child's treasure trove. There was a castle with soldiers on the ramparts that would have sent William delirious. 'So why don't you two get married and provide the next generation?' asked Carly. 'All these lovely toys lying here, waiting, giving no joy at all.'

'Which of us are you propositioning?' said Liam.

'Neither.' She was very emphatic. 'Not even to get a share in the dolls' house or a ride on the rocking horse. But it's a wicked waste, a room like this and no children in the house.'

'That's what Aunt Aimée's always saying,' declared Roland.

'Not to me,' said Liam.

'She's given up with you.' They were joking, and Carly guessed it was a family joke. Madame Corbé had no hope of Liam choosing one woman and forsaking all others, but Roland's children might play in here one day. They would be lucky. So would his wife; he was nice.

She stroked the smooth flank of the rocking horse and Roland told her, 'We've got a colt in the stables not much bigger than this. We'll start you on Mimi.'

'Couldn't I settle for this one?' It was so beautiful, in wood the colour of wet chestnuts, with a saddle that had once been scarlet leather and had aged to dark crimson. Carly slipped a foot in the stirrup and clutched the mane, and Liam put hands round her waist and lifted her up.

He was strong. She wasn't a featherweight girl, but she went up like a feather, and her fingers slid through the mane, her foot out of the stirrup, and over the other side she went, to land sitting hard on the floor. There was a shocked moment with both men asking if she was all right, before she began to laugh, 'I told you, that's how I am in a saddle. I slither off.'

If Roland had lifted her up she might have kept her seat, but she had automatically jerked from Liam's touch. 'You're sure you're not hurt?' He seemed concerned, and if she had been it could have been his fault.

She took Roland's hand to get to her feet. 'Not where it shows. Now,' she patted the rocking horse, 'steady, pal, because I'm going to try again, and this time, please, no hand-ups.'

The horse seemed high when she sat in the saddle and looked down. She moved to rock it and it creaked, then backwards and forwards, faster and faster, the noise of the rockers beating a brisk tattoo. It was fantastic. They must have loved it when they were children. It was big enough and strong enough to carry an adult's weight, but she was probably the only adult who had ever ridden it.

She was amusing them both. They were both laughing at her, carrying on like a child, but she was having fun, for the first time since she'd arrived here. If you closed your eyes you could imagine you were galloping away. But when she opened them Liam was watching her and she asked, 'Would there be any objection to me coming in here and playing with the toys? It's this retarded streak in me, the childish syndrome.'

She was half serious. She could have enjoyed herself. Few grown-ups can resist a toyshop, and this collection had the added fascination of the past. Roland smiled, 'Of course,' but Liam said, 'I wouldn't like Aunt Aimée to walk into the playroom and find you here alone.'

Alone as Antoinette, an only child, must have been many times, playing with the toys, riding the wooden horse. Carly slid off the still-moving horse and held it until it was motionless. She said, 'You shouldn't have let me. Where is she?'

'Downstairs,' said Roland.

Madame Corbé would know they were showing Carly round the house. She would half expect laughter, even the sound of a rocking horse. But if she found Carly alone in the playroom some time it might reinforce in her mind that fancied resemblance to Antoinette.

'I won't come in here,' said Carly. 'And just get me out of that bedroom, will you? I'm not her granddaughter, I'm nobody's granddaughter. So what can I do around here without you deciding I'm reminding her of Antoinette?'

She had hands on her hips, and her expression was mutinous. 'Just be yourself,' said Liam. He stood with folded arms, but his lips twitched. 'Tough as old boots.'

'You *what*? I am *not*!' she protested.

'Compared to Antoinette you are.'

'Compared to Antoinette I've had to be. It's easy to be gentle when you don't have to fight.'

'Oh, you poor darling!' Roland was instantly full of sympathy. 'Has it been that hard?'

'No.' She was explaining, not complaining. She thought, with a flash of intuition, that Roland had done very little fighting. It was Liam who went out and did battle, and because of that had a quick keen arrogance and no easy sympathy at all.

'How's your head for heights?' asked Liam.

'Average, I suppose. Why?'

'The view from the top of the tower's worth the climb.'

'Sure,' she said. 'Of course. Let's see if I can fall off that.'

This might be part of the truce, because open antagonism between them would upset Madame Corbé, but Carly was willing to be amenable if he was and she wanted to go up the tower.

But when he opened a door at the end of the corridor she looked through and gulped. She had expected steps, of course, but not as narrow and steep as these, going round the wall, with only a handrail barring a sheer drop into the well of the tower. The door opened straight on to the steps and she followed Liam out, glanced over at what seemed to be machinery a long way down there, and gripped hard on the handrail.

'Coming?' he asked. He was several steps up, and she was almost sure she was turning green.

'Of course I'm coming.' She clenched her teeth to stop them chattering and hoped it looked like a smile, and watched him go up, muttering, 'Has he ever fallen flat on his face?'

'If he has,' said Roland quietly, 'I was too far behind to see.'

'What do you mean?'

'As long as I can remember,' said Roland, putting out a hand to help her because she was climbing very slowly indeed, 'there's been no keeping up with Liam.'

'He's older than you, isn't he?' She wasn't exactly scared of heights, she just wasn't crazy about them, and this was enough to make most folk dizzy if they looked down.

'Four years,' said Roland, adding wryly, 'I'd have caught up with him by now if I was ever going to.

Sure you want to go up here? You are all right?'

Carly was grateful for his help, she would have hated to be doing this on her own. 'I'm all right,' she echoed, taking it step by step, looking up at the open trapdoor high above through which Liam had vanished, and wondering if she would have to come down backwards because she would never dare look down.

The stone of the wall felt clammy and slippery, but that was because her palms were sweating. She felt safer going up pressing against the wall, but her stomach muscles were starting to clench, and if that spread to her legs she could find herself paralysed with panic.

She started to chatter, asking what the tower was for. The answer was, nothing much. Farming and gardening equipment was stored in it and the room at the top had a splendid view. It had been built as a folly in the eighteenth century by an ancestor who liked to sit up there overlooking his estates.

'And wasn't much for company, I should think,' Carly muttered.

'You want to go the rest?' Roland asked. 'There is only the view up there.'

And Liam. She wasn't having Liam know that she was too scared to make it to the top. 'I'm all right,' she insisted. 'Truly,' and she moved a little faster to prove it. 'Once you get used to the feel of the steps it's easier.'

She was glad he was behind her and when they took the last bend there was Liam looking down. 'What kept you?' asked Liam.

'We came the pretty way,' she snapped. 'What do you think kept us? I came slowly and Roland stayed to help me. It's all right for you, but this is my first climb.' And her last. As she scrambled through the trapdoor she added sweetly, 'You wouldn't have liked me to slip, would you? I could have damaged a garden roller down there.'

'You said you had a head for heights.'

'Average, I said. And I didn't mean an average mountain goat.' It was lovely to be in a room with a floor. Her mouth was dry and her muscles were still in knots, and she dreaded the moment when she would have to go back through the trapdoor and start climbing down that great shadowy pit.

Up here the air seemed full of dancing gold dust. There were windows all around, and the sun came streaming in, so that even the floorboards had a pale yellow shimmer. The only furniture was a biggish table and a couple of chairs—fancy carrying a table up here!—and an old telescope on spindly legs, looking like some strange science fiction insect.

Liam went around the windows, rubbing briskly with a tissue and telling her, 'The rain cleans them outside, but you have to do your own polishing inside.'

Madame Corbé had said it was like being in the sky up here, and she was right. Carly felt that the little white clouds floating in the blue were almost within her reach. She began to rub a window pane for herself, and Roland said, 'Well? Aren't you surprised she made it?'

'No,' said Liam.

'Oh, come on!' Roland protested. 'How often does a guest get up here? Even the men?'

'True,' admitted Liam. 'But Carly doesn't give up easily.' She doubted if that was a compliment, and she looked round from her window pane starting to frown and he said, 'You'll be glad you came. I told you, the view's worth the climb.'

He took the brass cover from the lens of the telescope, and she put her eye to the eyepiece. It was muzzy at first but, as he adjusted, pictures came and went and she cried 'That's better ... yes ... no ... yes, it's getting clearer,' and finally in a yelp of delight, '*Yes*, oh, *marvellous!*'

A row of cottages sprang into sharp relief. She could see smoke rising from a chimney, black hens in a garden patch, and a woman in a red dress with a child beside her.

'I can see stone cottages,' she reported, moving the telescope a fraction and counting doors. 'One, two, three, four, five.'

'The farm workers' cottages,' said Roland. 'The Home Farm.'

'And a barn—a huge brick and timber barn. Is that part of the Home Farm too?'

'The estate covers fifteen thousand acres,' intoned Liam. 'Four hundred are the Home Farm, the rest is leased.'

'Fascinating,' she murmured, because he sounded as though he was quoting a guide book for her.

'I thought you'd like to know. There's also a canning factory belonging to the estate, four miles away. One tenant has a strawberry farm.'

Madame Corbé was a woman of property, and Roland managed her affairs. Carly said jokingly, 'I suppose you wouldn't consider a share in a small boutique?'

'She means it,' said Liam.

'We should discuss it,' said Roland, and Carly thought, Perhaps I do mean it. Liam was the obstacle, but the shop was a sound little business. Why shouldn't she try to help Ruth and William while she was here?

Thinking of William reminded her, and she enquired if there was a shop where she could get postcards to send home, and they moved the telescope round so that it peered into a street and she picked out shops and shoppers. Then she panned down to the beach, across the sward of sand and boulders, over the bright water. 'I've got an island,' she said. 'Is it the old chapel?'

She moved her head to let Liam lean over her shoulder and look through the glass. 'That's it,' he said, and she felt his breath on her cheek and put up her hand as though it was the touch of his lips she was warding off. Then she looked through the glass again and was transported to the island, so vividly that she could taste the sea.

The ruins were still recognisable. You could see the arches, the pointed ends of the roof, and the empty slit windows of the tower. It had been cut from the rock—which was pinkish on this coast—that was why it had weathered storm and salt so well. 'Can we go there?' she asked. The sea lapped around it. 'Is the tide going out?' It seemed that she was there already, standing on the shingle, but when she turned from the telescope and saw the gaping hole of the trapdoor she shuddered, 'Oh, my gosh, I'd forgotten I was up here!' She could feel herself stiffening and her voice came out jerkily. 'I don't know if I can make it down again.'

She expected Roland to understand, and Liam to say something like, 'You got up, you can get down,' amused at having manoeuvred her into a position of panic. She was breaking out in a cold sweat. If they had both left her—she knew they wouldn't, but if they had—she would have screamed and screamed. She would have shut the trapdoor on the steep steps and the deep drop and stayed up here, because there would have been no way she could have got down by herself.

'Take my hand,' said Liam, 'and don't look down.'

He went down a couple of steps and held a hand up for her, but she shook her head and edged herself through the trapdoor on to the first step. 'I'll take the rail,' she said. Her head was swimming and her stomach was churning, although she hadn't looked down; but she was convinced that she would be safer holding the rail than putting herself into Liam's hands.

'Close your eyes and count the steps,' he said. 'There are forty-three of them to the door into the house. You're on forty one now.'

Carly squeezed her eyes tightly shut and began to count, with Liam just below and Roland just behind. She felt the wall against her right shoulder, and the rail under the fingers of her outstretched left hand, as she went down step after step, like an automaton. When there were only five steps to go she opened her eyes briefly, then closed them quickly until Liam said, 'You're here,' and one of them turned her and she stumbled through the doorway and there was carpet under her feet.

She could have collapsed, her legs were jelly now from the reaction, as she sagged back against the wall, bitterly ashamed of herself, croaking, 'I never realised I should feel like that. I just wanted to get up, I didn't stop to think how much worse it might be coming down. I just seized up.'

She bit hard on her trembling lip, babbling, 'I never knew I suffered from vertigo. You learn something every day, don't you? I'd better wash my hands,' and she gripped her fingers together to control the shaking.

'What with last night and this I'm certainly looking my best on this holiday!'

'You're sure you're all right? Do you want to lie down?' Roland sounded very concerned, but it seemed that, having helped her down, Liam had used up all his solicitude. He said nothing and she smiled gratefully at Roland. 'Bless you—thanks, I'm fine. It's like seasickness, isn't it? Once you're on terra firma you're cured. I'll be back in five minutes.'

In the bathroom of the bedroom that had been Antoinette's she dabbed cold water on her temples and stood breathing hard, clutching the edge of the washbasin. That had been horrible, not just the physical sensation of sick helplessness, but making such a pathetic fool of herself in front of Liam, who was probably laughing about it right now.

She ducked her face into her cupped brimming hands, splashing water into her eyes, washing off the clammy perspiration, to come up blinking and gasping. When she saw Liam's reflection in the mirror over the washbasin she let out a shriek. He was in the bedroom, and she snapped, 'Don't you ever knock on doors?'

'Yes,' he said.

Perhaps he had. Carly grabbed a towel and began to dab her face. Pink lipstick came off on the white towel and she demanded, 'What do you want?'

'You are all right?'

'Of course. Did you think I'd dashed off to have hysterics in private?'

'It crossed my mind,' he said.

She was scared of him, following her into her bedroom, because she hadn't yet had time to get herself together and he might take advantage of that. It wouldn't be impossible. She knew it would be madness, but she felt it would be wonderful to be held in his arms and comforted. She put the towel back on the rail, and plucked a tissue from the tissue box to wipe off the remains of her lipstick. 'Well,' she spoke through stiff lips as she dabbed, 'I panicked. There's something else for you to chalk up against me. I'm a coward.'

'On the contrary,' he said. 'One thing I will grant you, you've got guts.'

'You're joking! I nearly went spare up there.'

'That's a steep flight of steps, coming down can be hairy if you're not used to them. But you pulled yourself together in record time.'

Because she was ashamed of being frightened. It had humiliated her, being helped down with eyes closed. She said, 'Well, I'll know next time. If anybody else asks me if I've got a head for heights I'll tell them "No higher than a double-decker bus".' She came out of the bathroom and went across to the dressing table, without taking her eyes off him, as though he had to be watched or he might spring on her.

'You want to go over to the chapel?' he asked.

'Yes, please, I'd like to.'

'It will be just you and me. Roland's been called into the office, something that has to be dealt with at once.'

She was suspicious. 'Did you fix that?'

'Why should I?'

To keep her and Roland apart? To get her alone without Roland? 'I wanted your brother to come along,' she said. Roland was her protector against Liam. And against herself.

'And you usually get what you want.' That was how he had thought of her ever since he had seen her in that court and heard Gerald's story.

'Don't you?' she flung back.

'More often than not.'

Much more. often, she thought, and remembered Victoria and Alison. The way Liam was looking at her now made her go hot and cold and her heart seemed to be struggling as though her rib cage was too small. He wanted her. He was cynical and sensual, and he would have her if she gave him half a chance.

'You wouldn't be afraid of me, would you?' he drawled, and Carly knew she was staring at him as though she was hypnotised. She threw back her head and said, 'Ha!' as if that was such a crazy idea; and then she said, 'Of course not, but I'm remembering that the last time you were in here, last night, you knocked me down, and that's making me a bit twitchy. So would you mind getting out of my bedroom so that I can get my lipstick on straight?'

'Of course,' he said. 'But can I put it on record that I didn't push you first? What did you expect me to do—turn the other cheek and get them both clawed?'

He was waiting for her downstairs in the drawing room. There was no sign of Roland, but Madame Corbé sat on the sofa with a red lacquered box beside her. 'You went up the tower? said Madame Corbé. 'That was very brave of you.'

'Brave?' echoed Carly. 'Did he tell you I came down with my eyes shut? I was paralysed! If they'd left me up there I'd have stayed and starved and ended as the ghost in the tower.'

'Not you,' said Liam.

Madame Corbé laughed. 'I don't believe that would happen. You wouldn't give up so easily. Now, look what I have here.' She put the box on her knee and opened the lid and Carly sat down beside her and said, 'Oh, how lovely!'

Liam was standing by one of the windows. He couldn't see what was in the box, and he didn't know. Carly could feel his eyes on her and she thought—he thinks it's jewellery. The box was full of buttons, pretty buttons, Victorian, Edwardian, no great value, but they made Carly's eyes shine.

'A present,' said Madame Corbé. 'For the exquisite blouses and dresses that you make.'

'Are you sure? Oh, I could have such fun with these!' Carly gloated.

Liam came over and Carly closed the lid and looked up at him with mischievous smugness. He asked, 'What are you handing over?'

'Buttons, dear,' said Madame Corbé, telling Carly, 'We used to keep them in the old days, and use favourite ones on new dresses. We had a dressmaker when I was a girl, living here. Her name was Berthe—oh, she was so clever.'

Carly opened the box again and showed Liam and said, 'Now you're sure it's all right? Would any of your lady friends like them? Perhaps you could get one of them stitching some on a shirt for you?'

Madame Corbé smiled at that and Liam said drily, 'My lady friends don't do much sewing.'

Carly could visualise a whole collection of shirt-blouses with the buttons giving them flair. She must tell Ruth about it, and she asked, 'May I phone home tonight?' Madame Corbé said yes, of course. 'Just to check that all's well, although I'm sure it will be. And I did promise William I would phone.'

'You're very fond of William, aren't you?' said Madame Corbé gently.

'He's a love, I'm going to get some cards to send to him. He thinks you're something out of a fairy tale, you know.' This wouldn't go down too well with Liam, but he suspected everything she did anyway, thinking she was grabbing something really valuable just now. 'Coming into the shop like that,' she went on, 'out of nowhere. He fancies a grandmother, he doesn't have one, and I said I'd ask you. I thought you lived all by yourself then, and I thought you might come round to our house in the evenings. Anyhow, I wonder if you'd just write 'grandmother' at the bottom of a card for him if I brought one back.'

But certainly Madame Corbé would be delighted. One of the photograph albums was still on a small table beside the sofa, and she said, 'Talking of children, do you know who this is?'

A small boy and a small fair-haired girl were sitting on two ponies. In the background was the barn Carly had spied through the telescope; she asked, 'Antoinette?'

'Of course.' Madame Corbé's face shadowed for a moment, then she smiled. 'But do you recognise the boy?'

'Roland.' She had known it was Roland right away. He looked a jolly little chap, smiling for whoever was taking the picture.

'It's a pity Roland is caught up in business matters this morning,' said Madame Corbé regretfully. 'I'm sure he would much rather be with you.'

'I'd have liked that too,' said Carly, and wondered what Liam had looked like when this was taken. There were several other photographs on the page, of Antoinette and Roland and the two fat ponies, all taken, she guessed, on the same day. She asked Liam,

'Where were you?' and Madame Corbé answered, smiling,

'He'd galloped off. There's never been any holding Liam, not even when he was a boy.'

'That doesn't surprise me,' said Carly.

'Postcards, you said,' said Liam. 'If you don't get them posted you'll be back before they arrive. Shall we go?'

As they came out of the Château through the main door he announced, 'We have a choice—down the cliff steps or by the road. The cliff steps are more direct but steeper.'

Carly shuddered. 'That's no contest! Please let's go by the road. Today is the kind of day I could get stuck half way down a cliff.'

'And stay there till you starve and then haunt the cliff face?'

'You wouldn't like that, would you? Me, here for ever?' She grimaced at him, eyes dancing. She knew he was dangerous, and could be destructive to her, but there were times when he filled her with gaiety, a desire to joke and tease, and carry on as though she wasn't a day over sixteen.

Liam pretended to consider, then said, 'Let's take the road,' and would have taken her hand, but she wasn't risking that.

The seafront of Guirec Vert was quite busy. There were tourists here. They were easy to pick out, shopping, sunning themselves. Several local people spoke to Liam, calling greetings, eyeing Carly, and she smiled and said '*Bonjour*,' and wondered what they were making of her.

One man came hurrying after them. He had come out of the pâtisserie, carrying a couple of long rolls

under his arm, and he called, 'Monsieur Sherrard!'
Liam stopped and waited, and when he reached him
the man began to talk in fast and worried fashion.

Carly moved away. She couldn't understand, but it
was obviously personal. She walked on to where the
notice Bar-Tabac was displayed and then looked back
and watched, and saw the man's face clearing and
thought, There's a problem being solved. He was
smiling when Liam left him. He shook Liam's hand
and went off, walking jauntily as though a weight had
been lifted from his shoulders.

It was no business of hers, but when Liam reached
her she asked, 'A client of yours?'

'In a way.'

'Do you charge, or give your legal services free
round here?' She had no idea why she asked that, but
Liam had looked concerned and involved in whatever
problem it was that the man had brought him. Not at
all like an inquisitor.

'Why?' he asked. 'Do you want some free legal
advice?'

She wouldn't have minded talking about the lease,
but she said, 'I don't trust free gifts. I knew a man
once who gave me presents and then I found I was in
deep, deep debt.'

He knew she meant Gerald, but she didn't want to
talk about Gerald, so she dived into the shop and began
to choose cards from the rotating display just inside
the door.

There were several of the Château des Sables. She
bought two of each of those, and another half dozen of
the coastline and the countryside, and took them up to
the woman at the counter, who smiled and said, 'You
are staying at the Château?' Liam was just outside the

window, she must have seen Carly with him.

'Yes,' said Carly.

'A friend of Monsieur Sherrard?'

She amended that to, 'A friend of Madame Corbé,' and wondered why she was bothering to stress it. She was sure the woman watched her walk off with Liam and was remembering other girls who had strolled with him along the seafront.

She sat on the low sea wall to write William's card, making a rough sketch of a flying lion, and printing underneath it, 'This is the Winged Lion of Guirec Vert. His name is Leo. I will tell you all about him when I get home.'

'Who says his name is Leo?' asked Liam, reading over her shoulder.

'Isn't it? Do they have names?'

'No.'

'Then why not Leo?' She pulled a face. 'Although he does look more like a flying pekingese than a lion.'

'Give him here.' Liam took the card and her ball-point pen, put his foot on the sea wall and balanced the card on his knee, and with a few strokes made the lion into a lion. Then he added a girl on the lion's back, hair flying, smirking smugly, and in the lower left-hand corner a recognisable pirate, booted and eye-patched, leaping around in comic rage.

Carly burst out laughing when he showed it to her. 'My, aren't you talented?'

'Oh yes,' said Liam. As she took back the card he leaned over and cupped her chin, tilting her face, and again she felt her blood leap. Her tongue flickered between dry lips and she thought, He's going to kiss me, and if he does I could kiss him back, and then he'll know and then I'm finished.

She said, 'I must post the card. How long will it take? I don't want to get home before it does. Is that likely to happen, do you think?'

'That depends on how long you're staying.' He wasn't going to kiss her after all. He made no attempt to stop her moving away, and she couldn't have said if she felt reprieved or let down.

'When are you going back?' he asked as they walked across to the postbox. 'I can give you a lift any time up to three weeks. That's my deadline, I have to report in three weeks.'

Carly had planned on a fortnight, but she could make it a little longer. She said, 'No, thank you,' dropping in her card. 'Coming here you were putting me through the third degree, weren't you? Dredging up anything that might discredit me.' He didn't deny it. 'So I'm doing no more travelling with you.'

'Pity,' he said cheerfully. 'I felt we got to know each other pretty well, but it could have been much more pleasurable on the way back. I might have surprised you with the extent of my talents.'

'No, thanks,' she said again, and turned her face towards the sea breezes, because she was sure she was blushing scarlet.

The mount of the chapel was only an island at low tide. The rest of the time it was the end of a rocky outcrop. Weeds grew in the crevices of the rose-red rocks and green pools glittered, but Carly resolutely refused a helping hand, and scrambled, slithered and jumped, getting along quite well and enjoying herself immensely.

There were a few tourists about, on the beach and climbing the rocks. On the causeway a middle-aged man was photographing a middle-aged woman who was perched rather stiffly on a small boulder, and Carly felt a fellow feeling for them. She was a tourist herself, and she wished she had brought a camera along. Postcards weren't the same, although she couldn't see herself asking Liam to take snapshots of her.

They didn't do much talking, but she knew that he was getting the same exhilaration as she was from the sparkling day. She said, 'You swim, of course.' Of course he did, this place was his second home. 'We must have a race some time,' she added.

'Any time.' He cautioned her, 'But remember the rocks.' With the tide out she could see what the smooth water would hide, and she smiled a little wryly.

'When your aunt said that I thought I'd do better to go swimming with Roland, I'd be safer with Roland.'

'That depends,' said Liam, and she might have asked what it depended on, but they were reaching the end of the causeway, where the island rose up in front of them, and she fell silent.

They stepped from the rocks on to a fringe of shingle and began to climb up the slope. Rough grasses covered the knoll and when she stood in the shadow of the ruins her exuberance gave way to hushed awe. The great rock arches were open to the sky and she went ahead of Liam, walking slowly, breathing deeply.

The sea stretched beyond, with a white boat on the horizon, and she stepped through a gap and stood with the wall at her back looking out over the waves.

Madame Corbé used to come here to be alone, but Carly wasn't alone. Liam hadn't spoken since they reached the island, and she hadn't heard his footsteps through the cries of seabirds and the sound of the sea. But she knew he was close and she said, 'Your aunt told me this used to be her favourite place. That she used to come here to sort out her problems.'

'Understandable,' he said, and he was near enough to have touched her. 'She's always been a great one for problems and plans. One problem she's working on right now.'

'What do you mean?' Carly's head jerked round. She suspected he was going to say something annoying, but what he did say shook her speechless.

'Oh, come on. Since you got here it must have dawned on you that she's planning to get you married to Roland.'

CHAPTER SEVEN

THE thought that Madame Corbé wouldn't mind if Roland and Carly took to each other had occurred to Carly, but she hadn't considered it as a permanent relationship. It was understandable that Madame Corbé should want the brothers, who were the last of the line, married, but Carly couldn't believe she would simply select a girl at random and expect Roland to settle for her choice.

She exclaimed, 'That's ridiculous!'

'Of *course* it's ridiculous.' Liam sounded as though it would be hard to find anyone less suitable, and Carly's eyes narrowed. 'I thought at first it was just this fancied resemblance to Antoinette,' he went on, 'that she might imagine she had a replacement and get hurt that way, but it now seems she's carrying it several stages further. Roland and Antoinette married would have been her dream, I suppose. The locals used to

call them the little sweethearts because they were the
same age and always together during the holidays, although it was a brother-sister relationship, the three of
us.'

'It might have grown into something else,' said Carly
quietly. Her face softened and her lips curved. She
could imagine Antoinette and Roland growing up together here and falling in love. It would have been like
a story, and she enjoyed a good love story.

'Antoinette has been dead for twenty years,' said
Liam harshly, jarring her romantic train of thought,
'so talking about what might have been is bloody
pointless. And this scheme of my aunt's is absurd.'

If he had been less scathing she would have agreed,
but instead she snapped, 'Well, I wouldn't expect you
to give it your blessing.'

'I'd go farther than that. I wouldn't allow it.'

How about that for ego? Who did he think he was?
Carly nearly fell about laughing, but there was something in Liam's expression that stopped her from
smiling, much less laughing. She felt the warm rock of
the broken wall pressing against her shoulder blades and
her voice was cold. 'Surely the problem is Roland's,
not yours. Anyway, why wouldn't you allow it?'

She knew the answers to that, but she was mad and
she wanted him to spell them out. That a shopgirl was
not taking over the ancestral home, especially a shopgirl with the record of Caroline Brown.

'You know why,' he said.

'Because I'm a peasant?' She grinned then, mocking
him, 'And your aunt found me in a little shop?'

'I couldn't care less where she found you,' he said.
'I know you could play any part you put your mind
to.'

She could act and look as well-bred as any of them, she knew that, but Liam judged her by what they had said about her when Gerald was on trial, and she said bitterly, 'But you don't think I'd be good for your brother because your lawyer friend made me out a gold-digger.'

'It's a point,' he admitted.

It was the main point. It was all Liam really had against her, and she could do nothing about it because he would go on believing what he wanted to believe. She watched the soaring leisured flight of a seagull. That kept her head up, and gave her a haughty look as though almost anything interested her more than he did.

'Looking for a winged lion?' he asked.

'Why should the winged lions be out today?' He was talking nonsense and so was she, but suddenly he was standing in front of her so that she couldn't look up or anywhere without looking at him, or move without touching him, and her entire body shivered. She said very quickly, 'What makes you think there's any risk that Roland would want to marry me?'

'Roland tends to let his heart rule his head,' said Liam, 'but it isn't going to happen, and you know why.'

Carly only knew that the full length of his body seemed pressed against her, disturbing her so that she was conscious of nothing else. His arms held her, against the wall, against him, and she knew that when his mouth covered hers it would be like a match set to paraffin.

'Hell,' Liam swore softly. 'Hell and damnation!'

'W-what?'

'Oh dear!' gasped somebody. 'Er—*bonjour. Pardon.*'

It was the middle-aged man and woman who had been taking photographs among the rocks, looking hot, and disconcerted at stepping through a hole in the wall and almost colliding with a pair locked in an embrace. Another few minutes and they'd really have been embarrassed, Carly reflected, blushing scarlet, and oh Lordy, so would she!

'Good morning,' said Liam. He kept an arm around Carly's shoulder and gave the arrivals a grin that had them smiling back. 'My fiancée and I were just admiring the view.'

The woman twinkled at Carly; she obviously thought they were a handsome couple. Carly's heart was thudding away and her head was beginning to throb with it. All she could manage was a fixed smile, standing stiffly in Liam's careless embrace, while he and the couple discussed the weather and the view. They were touring, they had stopped for a coffee and a walk on the beach. Were Carly and Liam touring? 'No,' said Liam, 'we're staying with friends.' Very nice, that was, said the woman. The man said these ruins looked old, did Liam know what they were? 'Just the remains of an old chapel,' said Liam.

'Well, enjoy your holiday,' they both said, stepping back through the wall.

'You too,' said Liam, and Carly gulped and said, 'Oh yes, have a lovely time.'

She would have to give them a few minutes to get ahead on the causeway. She needed a breathing space to pull herself together, she felt as shaky as though she had been plucked out of a raging sea. 'I wonder if his name's Leo,' said Liam ruminatively.

'Why should it be?'

'No winged lions appeared to save you. They could come in disguise these days.'

The intruders hadn't looked in the least leonine, more like a nice little pair of hamsters, but their arrival had halted what could have developed into some very passionate lovemaking. Carly said shortly, 'What rot you talk!'

'Think so? Five minutes later and I might have been saying, "My wife and I".'

'You would not!' she snapped. 'Did you really imagine I'd let you——' She waved furious hands, gesticulating revulsion, indicating the wide open spaces around; trying to express that as far as she was concerned this was neither the time, the place, nor the man. She practically spat at him, 'You're so conceited you're insufferable!' and then she stood back scowling.

'You're not exactly humble yourself,' he retorted. 'But you feel it too, don't you?'

'What?' She still scowled.

'That you and I could be sensational together.' Carly had never come across another man for whom she had felt such a consuming desire, but letting him love her would be as risky as running up the steps of the tower two at a time. She could fall a long way and end up very broken indeed.

There would be no danger for him. On the contrary, he could be reasoning that making love to her would stop her making a play for Roland. 'You must see that I can't let you marry him,' he said. 'I can't end up lusting after my brother's wife.'

He was joking. In a way. His mouth had a wry twist, and she said tartly, 'That might be uncomfortable for you,' but so long as she didn't feel the same not much harm could be done. 'And I don't even like you, much less lust after you.'

'Odd, isn't it?' he commented. 'You're not my type either.' He touched her wrist very lightly, and he must have felt her pulse racing there before she jerked her hand away. 'Another time?' he said.

It was useless protesting that she felt nothing, but her head was going to rule her heart. No, not her heart. Her heart wasn't involved either. Only her body wanted to make love with Liam more than anything else in the world. 'There isn't going to be another time,' she said shortly. 'Let's get back. I'd hate to get cut off here by the tide.'

'You mean with me?' Of course she meant with him. Alone, or with anyone else, it could be pleasant on a summer's day like this. She stepped through the broken wall and began to hurry towards the causeway, then laughed, 'Forget it—I'll swim,' and he laughed too, and she thought, this is like a sport to him, but if I ever let him run me to earth his talons could drain the life out of me.

Going back they took the cliff path from the beach to the Château. It cut off the longish walk round by road, and although it was steep it was nothing like the ascent of the tower. Carly managed the climb comfortably. As they climbed they talked, but discussed nothing of any importance. There was no further mention of Madame Corbé's hopes of pairing Carly off with Roland, and Carly was unconvinced. It sounded a highly unlikely set-up to her, but Roland was waiting for them. He came across the grass towards the cliff-edge as they toiled the last few steps, and she suddenly felt embarrassed, wondering if there *was* any chance that she was here for Roland's consideration.

As usually happened when she was ill at ease she

began to chatter. 'Hello, are you through with the work? We've had a super walk out to the chapel. It's fantastic out there. Well, you'd know about that, of course, but I found it terribly impressive, it fairly took my breath away.' She could say that again! Out there she had nearly stopped breathing and stopped thinking. She had nearly let Liam seduce her in broad daylight, and Roland said, 'The sun's caught you,' smiling into the warm guilty glow of her face.

'By the way,' said Liam, 'I met Jacques Nathan, and told him his son who's getting married next month could have the old Galaine cottage.'

'Yes, all right,' said Roland, agreeing as though he was taking instructions rather than being consulted, and Carly wondered why Liam was allocating cottages when Roland managed the estate. But it was none of her business. After the climb, in the heat of the day, she was anxious to get inside the cool house. Roland took her arm, crossing the lawns, and Liam strode along on her other side, and she thought, just suppose I am here on approval, and before I leave Roland does ask me to marry him. Suppose I said yes, then this is how we would walk—Roland holding my arm, Liam sometimes beside us. Crazily she wanted to reach out and take Liam's hand and warn Roland that she was unsuitable for the rôle which Madame Corbé might have in mind for her.

Madame Corbé was still in the drawing room, sitting with her feet up on the sofa. Carly thought she looked pale and Liam asked, 'Are you all right?'

'A little tired. Did you have a pleasant walk?' They said that they had. 'And did you get the postcards to send to William?'

'I sent him one,' said Carly, producing the others

from her shoulder bag. 'Would you like to write love
to him on this one for tomorrow?' She offered her pen
and one of the cards showing the Château, and
Madame Corbé wrote 'This is my home where Carly
is staying. Perhaps she will bring you to visit me, Love
from Grand'mère.'

'That's lovely,' said Carly. 'Thank you.'

'I haven't written "Grand'mère" for a long time,'
said Madame Corbé and Carly knew she was remembering Antoinette and wished she had never
promised William that she would find him a grandmother. She was undecided about sending the card.
This was another promise, and one that might be impossible to keep.

The box of buttons was on the side table by the
settee and Carly opened it and showed Roland, 'Look
what your aunt's given me. I'm going to make some
designs before I go back. Then if I start work in earnest
I might have enough for a Christmas display. Blouses
mainly, I thought.'

Madame Corbé leaned across and took out a tiny
square button, set with seed pearls. 'There should be
four of these,' she said. 'They were on a blouse that
was made for my trousseau,' and Carly exclaimed de-
lightedly,

'Like the blouse in the window? The one you were
looking at the day we met?'

'The very one,' said Madame Corbé. 'Have you
started making your trousseau yet?'

'No,' Carly smiled, shaking her head. 'It's not the
same these days. You just start sewing or buying when
the time comes.'

'Perhaps the time has come,' said Madame Corbé.
'Why don't you make a blouse for your trousseau?'

Her smile was roguish and she looked straight at
Roland after Carly.

Liam drawled,

'Carly's a career woman. She was suggesting earlier
that we might invest in her boutique.'

'Oh!' That took Madame Corbé by surprise. It took
Carly too. She protested,

'It was a joke.'

'You don't need investors?' Liam persisted, and she
hesitated. She badly wanted to say, 'No,' but she kept
thinking of Ruth and William, so she said,

'Well, yes, we do. Rather urgently, actually. But it's
a sound little business, and anyone would get their
money back. Not all at once, of course, but they would,
and with interest.'

'We'll have to look into it,' said Liam affably.
'Consider the collateral.'

Back to the beginning, she thought. Then it was,
'How much not to go to Guirec Vert?' Now it's, 'How
much to leave?'

Liam seemed to be more of a power here than
Roland was. His influence on them both was obviously
strong, and Carly said, 'I'm our collateral.' Liam's lips
twitched and hers tightened. The only service she was
offering was financial, let there be no mistake on that.
'I'd pay your cash back, believe me,' she added.

'What about the man who saw you off at the airport?
He seemed concerned for your welfare. Wouldn't he
like to back the boutique?'

Liam was enjoying this, and she said tartly, 'He's
got no money.'

'Well, well, so practically any offer was a better
one?'

She jumped up to walk out, and the box of buttons

spilled over her feet, over the carpet. In the confusion of gathering them up again, with Madame Corbé reminiscing as they were dropped back into the box, Carly's fury had time to fade. Scooping up the last button, a multi-faceted jet that had rolled across to the wall, Liam asked, 'How about it, Aunt Aimée? Would you like a share in a dress shop?'

'I think I might. It's a very attractive shop,' agreed Madame.

'I'll send someone round, then,' said Liam.

Almost surely there would be strings to this, but that was a risk Carly must take, she couldn't let the chance slip. She asked, 'Please may I phone Ruth?'

'Of course,' said Liam, and went with her to the nearest phone in the hall.

She would have preferred to talk to Ruth in private. He inhibited her. Just by standing there he reminded her that his was the final word. Ruth was at the shop, and Carly told her, 'Somebody will be calling you about the business. The family here may consider putting some money in.' Ruth's squeal came loud enough for Liam to hear. Ruth was a quiet girl as a rule, but now she shrieked, 'Wouldn't that be marvellous?'

'Wouldn't it?' said Carly. 'So—you know, show them around, show them the books and explain the potential.'

'Oh, I will, I *will*,' promised Ruth fervently. She giggled, 'Hey, you did find us that millionaire, didn't you?' Liam was standing almost shoulder to shoulder. Carly was fairly sure he had heard that too. She said hastily, 'Right, then, I'll ring off for now. Everything all right? Good. Love to William. 'Bye,' and as she replaced the receiver she faced Liam defensively. 'It would be a sound investment. I would pay you back.'

'Oh yes, you will,' he said, and smiled, but Carly knew that for her it was no smiling matter.

She went out through the front door and walked round the terrace back to the drawing room, praying as she walked, please let it work out, please let Ruth have this break, please don't let Liam set the price too high. When she reached the long windows they were slightly ajar and she pushed them wider to step into the room. Roland was alone, sitting on the sofa. He jumped as she walked in. 'I wasn't expecting you to come that way. You've made your call?'

'Yes.' She sat down beside him. 'Does Liam have the final word on financial matters? I mean, couldn't you or your aunt make small investments on your own?'

'Of course.' But if Liam advised against it Carly couldn't see much being done for Ruth's little business. She said slowly, 'This could be a bribe.'

'A *what*?' Roland's eyebrows quirked, he looked amused.

'A bribe,' she repeated. 'If I'll opt out, clear off. Liam has this idea that your aunt might have been shopping around for a niece-in-law when she saw me and decided I was like Antoinette. Liam says they used to call you and Antoinette the little sweethearts.'

'So they did.' He was silent for a few seconds and she turned to the button box, and began slowly stirring the contents with a forefinger. Then he admitted, 'It's a possibility. She's growing old. She wants me married. She wants to see children in this house again.'

'What do you want?' asked Carly.

This time he didn't hesitate. 'I'd like that.'

'Then why aren't you married?'

He shrugged. 'I've had one or two near misses.'

'Like Liam?'

He said emphatically, 'No, not at all like Liam. Liam never even comes near getting married.'

Madame Corbé must be reaching a state of near-desperation when it came to going out and bringing in Carly. At least that was how Carly saw it and how it struck Liam. She picked out a button like a crystal heart and thought what a romantic Madame Corbé must be. 'One of the reasons she asked you here might be because we got on so well that first evening,' Roland conceded. 'She was certainly pleased about us dating afterwards. She never stopped talking about you, how like Antoinette you were. It worried Liam.'

'It would.' The tiny crystal heart glittered in her palm like a tear and she asked, 'Do you always consult her about your girl-friends?'

'Of course not!'

'Do you consult Liam?'

'*No!*' But he listened to Liam and Liam would not allow it. Carly laughed a little; but gently, she didn't want to hurt him. 'Well, I tell you that no way would he have me as a sister-in-law.'

'He might change his mind.' She noticed he didn't say it wouldn't matter.

'That I can't wait to see,' she said.

'I like you very much,' said Roland. 'Suppose we do spend this holiday getting to know each other?'

'I hope we do.' Although he might not like her more for knowing her better.

'At the end we might even think about going along with Aunt Aimée's idea?'

'Oh, I don't know about that.' He sounded quite serious and she thought, Madame Corbé need not have bothered. You'd have proposed to somebody suitable soon if you're considering a stranger, just because your aunt likes her and you find her quite attractive.

She couldn't take it seriously herself. She wanted to laugh and say, 'It's a crazy notion, although when she had said that she had been furious with Liam for agreeing. She said, 'I'm not looking for a husband. As Liam said, I'm a career girl. If I wasn't hooked on my job would I get this thrilled over a box of buttons? Look at this one. Isn't it pretty?'

She opened her hand on the crystal heart. 'Would you have some paper? I might come up with an idea or two before lunch?'

Roland brought her a writing pad from a bureau and she sat herself at the big round inlaid table, while he sat down opposite as though he intended studying her at work. She said, 'I frown a lot. Apart from that there isn't much to watch.'

He smiled, telling her, 'Even when you're frowning you're the nicest thing to look at round here,' and she laughed,

'Well, I make a change. One thing against living with priceless heirlooms—I suppose you could get bored with them. My kind of home changes every time I pass a junk shop.'

'Wouldn't you like to live here?' Like Barney, only a few days ago although it seemed much longer, Roland was visualising her in his home and deciding she might not be out of place. At least she supposed he was.

She said, 'Who wouldn't? Such a beautiful house,' and thought, if I was offered the chance I don't think I would take it.

She began to sketch, and Roland watching didn't bother her. She concentrated completely on her design until Liam walked into the room. Without raising her head she knew who it was when the door opened, but she went on looking at the sketch on the pad as he leaned over her shoulder. 'Not your trousseau?' he queried. 'What is it, a nightshirt? Aunt Aimée will be pleased.'

'You're embarrassing her,' Roland protested, and Liam gave a hoot of derision.

'It would take more than that to embarrass Carly, wouldn't it, my beauty?' He smiled down into her angry eyes, and she said,

'Oh yes, you'd know that. You knew everything about me the moment you set eyes on me in court all those years ago. And that's why I've been explaining to Roland that you'd never accept me as a sister-in-law.'

'You're damn right I couldn't,' Liam agreed cheerfully.

'And that if you do put any money into Ruth's shop it will probably be on condition that I go home and keep away from your family.'

'*Ruth's* shop?' He pounced on that as though she had slipped up under cross-examination, admitting something that made all the difference. 'Aren't you partners?'

She was so alarmed she started stammering, 'No—I mean yes, we're partners, we work together, but she's the owner, it's her shop. Why? It doesn't matter, does it? With a little help I know I could keep things going. And paying. Ruth and William need that shop,' she pleaded. 'I could get another job, I can always sell my stuff, but they need the shop and I do desperately want to help them keep it.'

For the first time Liam looked taken aback. Then he

said, 'I presumed you were doing this for yourself.'

'I don't ask for things for myself,' she muttered.

'So it seems I don't know you as well as I thought I did,' and joy bubbled up inside her because he was believing her and because she suddenly believed he was going to help.

'About time you got round to admitting that,' Roland said jubilantly. 'Now how about forgetting what happened years ago? This is the first day of Carly's stay here, let's all get to know each other better, eh?'

But it wasn't the first day. She and Liam had travelled to Guirec Vert together and too much had happened. She had fought with him, she had almost made love with him. She could start afresh with Roland any time, but Liam was under her skin. They could never draw apart and start as strangers.

Liam didn't answer Roland, he didn't seem to have heard him. He asked Carly, 'Do you really want to get out of Antoinette's room?'

'Yes, I do.'

'Fancy moving into Napoleon's? I've explained to Aunt Aimée that he's one of your heroes.'

'He is *not!*' she protested. 'I don't like dictators. Anyhow, what about all the antique draperies?'

'No problem,' said Liam. 'We'll put the drip-dry up for you.'

'Right, then.' She pushed back her chair. 'I'll move right now if you're sure she won't mind.'

It was rather exciting to be moving into Napoleon's room. It didn't take long, she hadn't brought all that much with her, and Liam and Roland helped her carry her clothes from Antoinette's wardrobes and chests of drawers and put them into the dark oak closets.

'Bathroom next door,' said Liam, 'and we'll bring you in a mirror.'

There was no mirror. The dressing table would have to be either a table or an oak chest. 'Was Joséphine with him when he stayed here?' she asked, imagining a fire burning in the stone fireplace and the little Emperor and his Empress taking supper together.

'This was after Joséphine,' said Liam. 'And after the retreat from Moscow. He brought a small bodyguard and one of his generals.'

'Joséphine would have been nicer.' She sounded rueful, and Liam grinned,

'He'd probably have agreed with you.'

'Still, it's all very grand. I've never had a room like this before.' Carly ran her fingers down the carved post of the four-poster. There was still a faint impression on the damask coverlet where she had lain earlier today, when Liam had stood over her. She wanted to smooth it out, but she could hardly do that with both of them watching her. She looked away and around and Liam said, smiling, making a joke, 'What are you thinking about? That all this could be yours?'

He knew why she had turned from the bed. He knew it had nothing to do with any plans of Madame Corbé's. She said, 'That's a crazy idea, so shut up about it, will you?' Roland was protesting, placating, but whatever it was he was saying hardly reached her. She seemed to be getting tunnel vision and hearing on to Liam, where he stood lounging, cat-like telling her, 'Crazy it is. Just remember that.'

Then she heard Roland saying something about lunch and made herself look at him and managed to say, 'Lunch? Yes—lovely. I'm starving. All this climbing and walking.'

Madame Corbé didn't join them for lunch. Her place
was set, but the pleasant-faced woman who served the
meals said that she was having something on a tray in
her room. She was tired, she had said, and Carly asked,
'Does she do this often?'

'No,' said Roland, as Carly looked anxiously from
one man to the other. 'I'll give the doctor a ring,' he
added, 'and see if there's anything we should be knowing.'

The empty chair took away Carly's appetite and as
soon as she could reasonably put down her knife and
fork she asked, 'May I go up and see her?'

'Of course,' said Liam. 'By the way, do you want
William's card posted?'

She hesitated, then decided, 'No, thanks, I think I'll
hold on to it. It's that bit about him coming here for a
holiday. He'd take that for a promise and maybe I
couldn't keep it, and children expect promises to be
kept.'

'Didn't we all?' said Liam. 'It's something we grow
out of.'

'I suppose so,' she had to agree, adding wistfully, 'A
pity, though.'

Roland took her up to Madame Corbé's room, which
was just along the corridor from Antoinette's room,
knocked on the door, looked in and said, 'We missed
you at lunch. Carly's come to sit with you for a while.'

Madame Corbé lay on a sofa under the window, with
some cold chicken and a salad that looked almost
untouched, on a table beside her. 'Anything wrong?'
asked Carly, and she smiled, 'Of course not, I'm just—
tired, but come in my dear, come and sit down.'

Antoinette's photograph in the oval silver frame was
beside the bed. Carly sat in a small button-backed chair

and Madame Corbé said, 'Liam says you want to move into Napoleon's room.'

'Not that room in particular.' Carly looped hands over her knees and her eyes were grave and troubled. 'But I didn't feel I should be in Antoinette's. Liam told me no one else has ever slept in there and it doesn't seem right that I should try to take her place. I couldn't, you see. Never. Because I'm somebody else.'

'Of course you are, my dear.' Madame Corbé looked across at the photograph and said gently, 'But in many ways you remind me of her, and isn't it natural that we should like those who bring back memories of our loved ones?'

Yes, it was natural, and it would have been untrue and unkind to deny it. 'I remember——' Madame Corbé began, and Carly hadn't the heart to stop her, so she sat and listened to stories about Antoinette and smiled and thought what a golden childhood that must have been.

'They used to call Roland and Antoinette the little sweethearts,' mused Madame Corbé, looking happy and animated now. 'Liam was always self-sufficient, even as a boy he never really needed anybody, but Roland and Antoinette seemed made for each other.'

How could they be at nine years of age? Carly wondered. It was fairy-tale stuff, all dreams. She said, 'Liam told me that,' and went on in a rush, 'He also told me something else.' This was going to be very embarrassing, but she stammered on, 'He said—er—that maybe you asked me here because you thought that maybe Roland and I——' but her words trailed away when Madame Corbé asked brightly,

'And why not?'

Carly had to set things straight right now. She

stopped stammering and tried to sound reassuring. 'I'm sure Roland is going to settle down soon. He told me himself that he'd like to be married, he'd like to have children.' Madame Corbé was alight with delight and Carly went on hurriedly, 'But it won't be me. We're worlds apart, and we hardly know each other.' Liam knew her best, and Madame Corbé would have been horrified at the things that Liam knew.

Carly stood up and said, 'I think I ought to go home.'

'Oh no! Please...' Madame Corbé was grasping Carly's hand in her surprisingly strong grip. 'All I'm asking is that you both give yourself a chance to get to know each other.' That was what Roland had suggested, but Carly's instinct had been to recoil. Just as it was now. 'Now that's all. Now that isn't too much to ask, is it?' Madame Corbé's breathing was quick and shallow, her lips were trembling, and how could Carly say, 'Too much, forget it?'

She had to admit, 'No, I suppose it isn't. But please don't upset yourself. I'm sure it won't be long before you'll have grandchildren around you.'

'Are you?' whispered Madame Corbé, and her eyelids fluttered. 'But I am so very tired.' She doesn't believe she has much time left, thought Carly, and a lump rose in her own throat that hurt when she spoke.

'You must rest,' she said gently. 'I've kept you talking. Close your eyes now.'

Madame Corbé lay back with a cushion behind her head and Carly gently smoothed the tendrils of hair away from the pale brow, then waited, sitting quietly, until Madame appeared to be sleeping.

Roland was pacing the hall and Carly hurried down the stairs to ask, 'Did you speak to the doctor?'

'Yes,' he said. 'How does she seem to you?'

'Exhausted. Of course she's not young. Is she often like this?'

'Only recently. She always had loads of energy.' They walked towards the open door of the drawing room where Liam stood at a window, his back towards them. 'Louis says,' said Roland, 'that this obsession that the family could end is putting undue strain on her heart. She's reconciled to Liam staying a bachelor, but he says the best treatment he can suggest is that you and I try falling in love.'

Liam walked out on to the terrace and Carly said desperately, 'It doesn't have to be us. She'd settle for any girl she believed would make you a good wife. Oh, why did you let the near-misses get away?'

'Well, right now,' said Roland, 'I'm going upstairs to tell her that I think you're a smasher and that we're getting on like a house on fire.'

It worked. Madame Corbé came down to dinner looking rested and wanting to hear what everybody had been doing all afternoon; and Carly wondered uneasily just what Roland had told her earlier, because when the time came for her evening constitutional around the terrace she said, 'Liam, shall we leave Roland and Carly alone for a while?'

Liam had been reading. He looked up from his book to ask, 'Why?' and Madame Corbé said plaintively, 'Because they might like to be alone. They might have things to discuss.'

'Nothing, I hope, that we can't hear,' said Liam. But he got up and put her shawl round her shoulders and offered her his arm, and as they walked off together Carly hissed, 'What does she mean—things to discuss? She isn't suggesting you propose to me tonight, is she?'

'That's what she'd like,' Roland chuckled. 'But I gather you wouldn't?'

'I'd think we'd all gone mad,' she said. 'If I'd had any idea I was putting myself—and you—into this position, I'd never have come here. I was so near saying no, thank you.'

'You were, weren't you?' He was remembering her reluctance. He asked, 'Why did you come?' and she said,

'Because you made it all sound lovely,' adding the real reason, 'And because Liam ordered me to stay away.' She grimaced, 'This is pretty awful for both of us, isn't it? Can you stand two weeks of it? Don't you think I ought to leave tomorrow?'

'Not at all,' Roland said hastily. 'My only regret is that two weeks will pass too quickly. Don't be embarrassed. Don't let this spoil your holiday.'

In a way the days did pass too quickly. After that evening nobody pressured her at all. Madame Corbé seemed content to see Carly and Roland—and Liam—always together and obviously in high spirits. Roland kept up a light flirtation, which proved what Carly had realised from the beginning, that he was a charmer; and Liam was the most stimulating companion she had ever known. She had a wonderful holiday.

She sent a daily card to William, which was rather like keeping a diary. 'Today they put me on a horse called Mimi and I fell off.' She had approached the stables with trepidation, wearing jeans and jumper and sneakers and protesting that she wasn't all that keen on learning to ride, but Mimi seemed a reassuringly docile animal.

Carly stroked her nose and fed her a lump of sugar and was glad she was so much smaller than the two huge prancing steeds that had also been led out of the stables. Mimi stood quite still while Carly was shoved up into the saddle, working her feet into the stirrups and being shown how to hold the reins. 'What do I do when she moves?' she asked, trying to smile.

'You'll soon get the rhythm,' said Roland. 'Move with the horse.'

That was unnecessary advice because the moment Liam and Roland turned away to mount their own horses Mimi threw back her head with a little whinny as though answering a distant rallying call, and moved off at a brisk trot.

Liam called, 'Pull her up!' but Carly promptly lost the reins, bouncing high and hard and scared out of her wits, until Liam galloped alongside and leaned over. As soon as the horse felt a firm hold on the rein she stopped dead and Carly, who by now had lost the stirrups as well, rolled off with all the grace of a sack of potatoes.

It was like the rocking horse all over again. And the donkey at the village fête. She was out of breath, shaken silly but unhurt, and as Liam and Roland jumped down beside her she hiccuped and began to giggle. It was nearly hysteria, but she caught that back and bit her lip and said, 'I told you. There's something wrong with me. I just don't have the right rhythm.' But she got the knack of it in the days that followed, and most mornings the three of them rode together over the countryside.

Roland's wife would ride, of course, better than Carly ever could, and she hoped he didn't imagine he was grooming her for the part of future mistress of the Château des Sables. But there was no further mention of that, not even by Madame Corbé, and staying here Carly met girls who seemed to fit the bill far better than she did.

Visitors called. There were dinner parties. There were girls who were young and attractive and unmarried, and good luck to them, thought Carly. After the first week she was sure that the idea of a match between Roland and herself had blown over, but she would have a tale to tell Ruth when she got back home.

She had spoken to Ruth a couple of times on the phone. When Liam returned to England there would be a conference about the business, and it really looked as though Ruth's boutique was going to get some backing. This was what the two girls talked about. Carly could hardly say on the Château phone, 'Guess why Madame Corbé got me out here. She wanted Roland to ask me to marry him, because I've got hair the colour of her granddaughter's.'

When she did say that Ruth would ask, 'Did he?' and be disappointed when Carly said, 'No.' And then Carly would have to explain that it wouldn't have worked, it couldn't have happened, and Ruth would shriek, 'Who are you *waiting* for? What do you want out of life?'

The Château was beautiful, magnificent. So was the countryside and the life they lived here. But Carly couldn't imagine growing old with Roland. This was a holiday romance, a brief and pleasant encounter with no future at all.

'I sleep in Napoleon's room,' she wrote to William. 'He was a soldier, very brave and very fierce, and he stayed here a long time ago.'

She slept soundly each night after happy and hectic days. Keeping up with Liam's idea of a holiday was no easy matter, but it was exhilarating. And so was he. He made her laugh at almost everything. He was a mine of information and a powerhouse of energy, but he made no demands and no passes, although there were times when Carly at least was so aware of the sexual electricity between them that she had to move away, because it made her feel dizzy.

Most days they swam—usually around the island of the chapel—and this she was really going to miss when she was back home. She learned where the rocks were. You could see them below in the clear water, the ones far enough down to be safe, the danger-rocks just beneath the surface. Roland let her win when they raced, but Liam wouldn't. It amused him to see her furious determination when he turned his head and saw her coming up behind him, and why she tried Carly didn't know. Her two weeks were nearly up and she was never going to swim faster than he could, but she still couldn't resist calling, 'Race you!' as they ran into the waves.

They always swam to the far side of the island and sometimes sunbathed on the turf under the ruined wall. This afternoon Roland and Liam were sunbathing and Carly was swimming, floating, playing around in the warm sun and the cool water—alone, she thought—when suddenly her ankle was seized and she was pulled down into the depths, hands outflung and hair streaming up.

Then her ankle was loosed and Liam's shimmering face was level with hers. He smiled at her through the water, then drew her close and kissed her mouth with cold hard lips, and they floated to the surface hand in hand.

'You idiot!' she spluttered. 'I thought a sexy old octopus had got me!'

'You should be so lucky!' They swam back laughing

and Carly scrambled up the shingle, up the turf, to Roland, gasping, 'Did you see that? He nearly frightened me to death!'

She hadn't been frightened. The underwater kiss had been fun. She sat down, shaking water out of her hair, tingling and glowing from head to foot, still feeling Liam's arms around her.

'Oh, I'm going to miss this,' she chattered. 'This time next week it will be the local pool for me.'

'Why not stay on?' Roland reached across for her hand. 'Marry me and stay on,' and she realised that he wasn't smiling.

She gulped, struck dumb. She had thought they had agreed that the matchmaking was preposterous, but he must have been assessing her day after day, and he believed she had been sizing him up too. He was in earnest. It was crazy, but he was.

'Oh no!' she stammered. 'Oh, I don't think so.'

'It's not a bad offer.' He still had her hand and she was hating hurting him. She said hastily and effusively,

'It's an absolutely terrific offer. Believe me, there's nothing personal about this. I do like you very much, I think you're one of the nicest men I know and I do love it here—well, who wouldn't, it's a beautiful house, a beautiful place—but—oh, can't you see that the idea's crazy?'

Liam suddenly loomed over them, as Roland said, 'So you said. That it was crazy. Why is it crazy?'

'Because——' Carly began desperately.

'Because,' drawled Liam, 'Carly and I are lovers. We slept together on our way here, and most nights since. Which might not make her marrying you crazy, but it would make it something of a calculated risk.'

CHAPTER EIGHT

CARLY felt punch drunk. She wanted to scream, but it
came out in a croaking gasp, and Roland dropped her
hand and jumped to his feet as though she had become
radio-active. He laughed savagely, 'Oh, my God, what
a fool I've made of myself! No wonder you wanted her
to move bedrooms!'

Antoinette's room was in another wing, but
Napoleon's room meant that Carly and Liam were next
door with Roland just along the corridor. 'Oh *no* . . .'
Carly began, but Roland wasn't listening, to her or to
anybody. He ran from them, plunging into the sea and
pulling away in a fast furious crawl, reminding her how
Barney had rushed down those steps in Birmingham
airport. Liam certainly knew how to make men hell-
bent on getting away from her, and she said bitterly,
'By the time he's swum to shore he should have washed
off my degrading touch.'

'He should have cooled down.' Liam sounded cool,
although what he had just done was monstrous. If she
and Roland had been falling in love a lie like that would
have poisoned everything, because she couldn't prove
it was a lie.

Roland envied Liam. There was a close brotherly
link between them, but Roland thought Liam was the
winner with women, with everything. He might not
have been swayed by arguments that Carly was a gold-
digger—he might have made up his own mind on that,
since he'd spent time in her company—but he would

167

believe that she and Liam were lovers.

She watched Roland's dark head, the lift of his arms, and thought, my heart could be breaking. It wasn't, because she wasn't in love with him, but she felt sick with misery and she said harshly, 'You need not have bothered to lie, I wasn't accepting.'

Liam just said, 'It was a risk I daren't take.' No apology, and no explanation except that obviously he hadn't changed his mind about her. All this holiday when she had fooled herself that they were friends he had still been watching her, protecting his family against her.

He didn't have to 'save' Roland. Carly could have extricated herself from that without a scene, and now there could be all sorts of unpleasantness and she was only thankful that she was leaving tomorrow. She wished she could leave now. Lord knows what she would have to face when she got back to the Château. Roland thought he had been cheated and fooled and there could be the most almighty row.

She got up. She felt old and tired, and her limbs seemed so heavy that she wondered if she could manage the swim back to the mainland. But she couldn't stay here till the tide went out. She would rather drown than stay with Liam, and he showed no sign of moving. He looked at her stone-faced, and she wanted to hurl her contempt at him. She should be boiling with anger, but instead she was shivering with cold, every emotion but misery drained out of her.

She muttered wearily, 'Oh, to hell with you!' then walked to the water's edge and waded in, and began to swim. The water buoyed her, cradling her. She was a strong swimmer, this was no distance, but she swam blind, less from the salt spray than from the tears that were pouring down her cheeks. If she had to weep this was the time. Once she reached dry land she must stay dry-eyed.

When she realised Liam was swimming beside her she jerked her head away and when he touched her she went to dive. 'Look where you're going!' he shouted, and the rocks were just below. After that Carly kept her eyes open, but as she waded out of the water blood began to seep from a graze on her smooth brown thigh.

They always left towels and clothes in a crevice in the rocks. She dried herself hastily and sketchily and dabbed the graze, wincing as it started to smart. She hadn't noticed brushing against a rock. She could have ended up lacerated to the bone if Liam hadn't warned her, but she still had nothing to thank him for.

Roland was on the cliff path, almost at the top. Carly saw him when she looked up and said, 'I hope he pushes your face in.'

'No danger,' said Liam. 'If he'd been going to he'd have tried it right away.'

She would deny it, of course. She would insist on being heard and it was unforgivable of Liam putting her in this position. She pulled her shirt over her head and tied the thongs of her sandals. The graze was superficial, but jeans would chafe it, so she carried them with her towel, and strode off across the beach, the thin white cotton shirt showing the wet pattern of her green bikini.

Liam was barefoot, bare to the waist, wearing jeans, towel slung around his neck, and other days when he and Carly had climbed the cliff after their swim he had given her a helping hand. Nearly always they had reached the top with Liam hauling her the final stage, both of them laughing. Roland was always with them, swimming and climbing and laughing, but Carly realised now how completely Liam had overshadowed him.

'Carly,' Liam began suddenly, and she burst out, 'Just don't talk to me. I wish I'd never set eyes on you or your rotten family!' She didn't mean it about his family. Roland had done her no harm and Madame Corbé was a darling, but she meant it about him. She went ahead up the cliff path, trying to pretend she was alone but agonisingly conscious with every step of him at her back.

When they reached the Château she ran to her room. If she had met anyone she couldn't have spoken to them. She was breathless from climbing the cliff and choked up with emotion, and she dashed into her bedroom and locked the door.

Although she was leaving the next day she hadn't yet started packing. It wouldn't take long and she supposed she hadn't really wanted the holiday to end, but now she opened her suitcase and began to unhang clothes from the closet, as though the sooner she packed the sooner she could leave.

That was stupid, and it was stupid standing around, sticky wet, her hair in rat's tails. After her swim she always showered and washed her hair in the bathroom next door, and she had to open the bedroom door again, looking up and down the corridor before she crept out to scuttle into the bathroom.

This afternoon she didn't linger. After her shower she dabbed the graze on her leg with antiseptic cream and was back in her bedroom within minutes, blow-drying her hair, then putting on the clothes she had set aside for this afternoon. The plan had been that they should drive into a town about ten miles away where she could do her last-minute gift shopping, but she couldn't see Roland wanting to join her and Liam now, and she was going nowhere alone with Liam ever again.

She would much prefer to spend the rest of this day on her own. She didn't know whether she could trust herself yet to say her piece. That Liam had lied. He and she had never even kissed, much less slept together, night after night, in that bed over there where Napoleon had once slept, at the end of his glory without much ahead but the years of his exile.

I bet he felt no more depressed than I do, Carly thought. This hurt more than when Gerald had let her down. She could remember that well, but she knew this pain would be worse when she let herself feel it.

Her dress was straight and simple in tangerine silk, with a matching cord jacket, and a scarf in tangerine cerise and scarlet, and she wondered how she could look so colourful and feel so drained. She dabbed more blusher on to her cheeks, although the suntan hid her pallor and the added pink looked feverish. She was rubbing it off when Madame Corbé walked in.

'You've started your packing?' queried Madame. The case was open on the floor and the closet door gaped. 'I shall miss you, my dear. I suppose you can't——'

'No,' said Carly jerkily. 'Thank you, but I must go.'

'Yes, of course.' The little swinging mirror standing on the dark oak chest had been brought in for Carly and Madame Corbé blinked at it. All her life this house had probably been unchanged in any way, so that even a mirror, where no mirror had been, surprised her. 'I've just seen Roland,' she said, watching Carly in the mirror. 'He seemed very annoyed. He said he had made a fool of himself and did I know about you and Liam. What could he have meant by that?'

'Nothing,' said Carly. 'There's nothing to know. Except that Liam doesn't like me and would move heaven and earth rather than let Roland marry me.'

'But he must like you,' Madame Corbé protested, as though Carly must be mistaken. 'He's been with you all the time. Liam doesn't suffer fools, or people who bore him. If he hadn't been enjoying your company he wouldn't——'

'He's been chaperoning Roland,' said Carly ironically. She had dropped a dress on the bed. She picked it up and folded it to fit the case, and Madame Corbé sat down on a carved high-backed chair, her fingers, with their flashing rings, playing with the gold rope chain she wore. 'Do you want to marry Roland?' she asked Carly.

'No, thank you,' said Carly promptly. 'Nor does he want to marry me.' . . . 'Stay and marry me,' he had said, but that offer had been cancelled by Liam's lies and if Carly had wanted to marry him she would have been distraught.

'I got the impression,' Madame's bright gaze switched from Carly's reflection to Carly, 'that he believed Liam was cutting him out in your affections.'

'Then you both have the wrong impression,' said Carly crisply.

'Roland is a dear boy,' said Madame Corbé as though she hadn't heard that. 'He would probably be happy with any girl so long as she was pretty and kind and loved him. But it would take a very special girl to hold Liam.' She nodded, agreeing with herself, and Carly rammed a rolled-up pair of tights down the side of the case and thought, special? She'd have to be a saint! And a fool, because falling in love with him could be bitter and terrible.

'As soon as I saw you,' mused Madame, 'I knew that you were special,' and Carly looked up wordlessly. This was beyond everything. She couldn't listen to this, and if Madame ever mentioned it to him it would be the ultimate insult for Carly. She could hear him laughing, saying, 'Not a good idea, my beauty.' She gulped and said, 'Liam isn't likely to fall in love. He's probably the most heartless man I've ever met,' and Madame laughed softly.

'Oh no—oh, you're wrong there. He's hard, but he can be wonderfully protective. There's nobody quite like Liam.'

'That's something,' Carly muttered. 'One's more than enough,' but Madame Corbé was enthusiastically away.

'And he's so clever. He owns most of this estate, you know.' Carly hadn't known and she didn't care. 'And he's a very successful lawyer—well, you know that.' Now Madame seemed to be talking to herself as much as to Carly. 'Of course he's never shown the slightest sign of wanting to get married. I never thought he would, although there've always been girls, and some of them were very nice. I didn't care much for the last one, Victoria, she was altogether too gushing, but you—now it would be simply splendid if you and he——'

'*Stop* it!' Carly shrieked. 'Stop it, I can't stand it! It was bad enough you matching me up with Roland just because you thought I looked like Antoinette. But the idea of trying to foist me on to Liam is obscene! We can't stand each other. I know we've been around together, and thank you for a lovely holiday, but when I get back to England he's the one man I hope never to see again. I'm sure he's super with you, he looks after his own, but what he's been doing with me the past two weeks is making sure little brother is safe. And I wouldn't have married Roland anyway, but I'd fifty times rather have him than Liam. I'd rather have nobody any time than Liam. Do you hear me?' Her voice had stayed at shriek pitch, but she hadn't realised what a shrill performance she was giving until she stopped for breath and saw Madame Corbé looking as astonished as if a box of fireworks had gone off in front of her.

'Sorry,' Carly ran a hand through her tumbled hair, 'I'm sorry, but you do hear?'

'I should think the whole house heard,' drawled Liam from the open doorway, and Carly's face burned as she turned away.

Madame Corbé said shakily, 'Carly's packing. It would have been nice if she could have stayed a few more days.'

'Wouldn't it?' said Liam.

'Would you get me a glass of water?' The old lady sank back in her chair breathing fast, and Liam poured water from a carafe by the bed while Carly stood transfixed with remorse. She shouldn't have carried on like that. She knew Madame Corbé wasn't strong and mustn't be upset. What had she done? 'My pills,' Madame Corbé whispered, and Carly jumped.

'Where are they?'

'In my purse. On the sofa in my bedroom.'

Liam was holding her hand, his fingers on her wrist. He said conversationally, 'I had a talk with Louis the other day,' and Madame's fluttering eyelids steadied.

'My doctor?' she murmured.

'Right,' said Liam crisply. 'He's the doctor, I'm the lawyer. He'd make an honest witness under cross-examination.'

The corners of Madame Corbé's mouth went up in a small mischievous smile. 'How very indiscreet of him!' She hadn't taken a pill, nor even drunk the water, but her voice sounded stronger.

'This,' said Liam, tapping the pulse point on her wrist, 'seems all right to me.'

'I do hope,' said Madame, 'that you didn't bully Louis.'

Carly waited and Liam told her, 'My lady here has had a heart murmur for years, but under slight pressure Louis admitted it's no worse than it was ten years ago and he thinks she'll see ninety.'

Carly didn't know whether she was shocked or amused, but she knew she was relieved. She gasped, 'You haven't been playing us all up? Trying to blackmail Roland into getting married by pretending you were ill?'

'Now I never said that,' Madame protested. 'Did I ever say I felt ill? I said I was tired, and so I was. Tired of waiting for him to choose a wife so that there would be children again, to play in the nursery and brighten up the place, and whatever my doctor says I am an old woman, I don't have that much time, I am seventy-five.

'First I saw my trousseau blouse in the window and that started me thinking about weddings.' She sighed wistfully. 'And then it was my birthday. Do you have any idea how many roses make seventy-five? I had one for every year.'

'Sorry about that,' said Liam, 'but it seemed a good

idea at the time,' and Carly remembered the yellow roses in Madame Corbé's bedroom in Liam's house. He must have arranged for them to be delivered, which was thoughtful, but seventy-five was a lot of years and roses.

She said gently, 'You'll see the children. They'll ride the rocking horse and rearrange the furniture in the dolls' house, even climb the tower with someone to hold their hands, and they'll be pretty and bright.' She wondered why painting that homely picture should make her feel so lonely.

'I hope so,' sighed Madame, 'but I still think it's a pity——' She looked at Liam, then sighed again and got to her feet. 'Ah well, I do hope Roland won't be still sulking tonight. We've got people coming to dinner, but he did look extremely put out.'

As soon as she was out of hearing Carly said, 'I can't believe it! She was so pale, she looked so ill.'

'Lack of rouge?' Liam suggested. 'She's genuinely anxious to see some prospect of another generation, but so far the suspense isn't killing her.'

'I'm glad about that.' She moistened her dry lips. 'I'm sorry I yelled at her, but I had to make her understand.'

'And I'm sure you did.' He sounded almost bored. 'It's as well Roland wasn't up here.' To hear Carly screaming how much she preferred Roland to Liam. 'Obscene,' she had said. The idea of loving Liam was obscene.

She couldn't look at him. She picked up her case and put it on the bed so that she could keep turning away to the closet, taking out clothes, asking him, 'Why did you tell him we were lovers anyway? I thought you'd decided that I wouldn't necessarily have been the worst wife in the world for your brother.'

He said slowly, 'When I first saw you you were in the witness stand, being questioned about the gifts and money you'd had from Gerald Collett,' and Carly stared into the dark recess of the cupboard, her back to him, reliving the moment she had looked up into the public gallery at Liam Sherrard.

'I thought then,' he said, 'that I could understand how he'd arrived where he was. You were a girl a man might do most things for, short of murder.'

'Just looking at me you thought that?' But she had looked at him, only fleetingly, and known him again years later. The impression they had made on each other in that courtroom had been searing.

'I've changed my mind slightly since,' he told her, 'but I'm still convinced you'd be disastrous for Roland.'

Disaster was a big word. Carly tried to laugh. 'You don't mean I could blight his life? If you do no wonder you didn't give me a chance to say yes when he asked me to marry him!' She picked up a small ornament that had come from the shop that sold postcards, and might be a present for someone back home, and dropped it into her case, then asked, 'How could you be sure that Roland wasn't coming to my room at night?'

Liam shrugged. 'I took a chance there. And I'm a light sleeper, I'd have heard anyone walking the corridors.'

Again she pretended to laugh, and again she failed. She said, 'As Roland said, no wonder you wanted me moved from Antoinette's room! You've put a guard on me all this holiday, haven't you? Just like you said you would. You keep your promises, don't you?'

'I try.'

He was cold and handsome and arrogant, and she wondered if she had put paid to the help that had been promised for the boutique, because she had shouted her opinion of him for anyone to hear. She asked fearfully, 'What about Ruth's business? When we get back are you still going to discuss——?'

'Don't worry, we won't have to meet. The arrangements will go through.'

'Thank you.' When she did look straight at him she could feel the pull like the tug of invisible cords that could have had her stumbling towards him. When she looked at him she ached for him, and he said, 'Strictly paperwork. No ex-gratia payment required,' and she thought, he knows it and he feels it, and the sooner I get away from him the better.

'One other thing,' she said. 'Please don't come with me to the airport tomorrow.'

'As you wish.' Liam closed the door behind him and Carly sank down on the bed beside the open case, her head in her hands.

Both Roland and Liam were supposed to be driving to the airport with her. She was flying back from Dinard, much nearer.

She picked up the little ornament she had just dropped into the case and balanced it on the palm of her hand. It was the small stone carving of a winged lion, a tourist souvenir that Liam had bought for her yesterday.

William would like it. Ruth had rung through the night before and put William on the phone, because his postcard, with the sketch of the lion flying away with the rescued maiden, had arrived that morning and William had worked out the story. He wanted to know why the lady had left the nice pirate behind. William liked the pirate, who didn't want to be on his own. Wasn't the lady mean?

Carly had laughed and repeated this for Liam, and Liam had said, 'Perhaps she'll go back for him.' So Carly had told William, and yesterday Liam had produced the lion and said, 'To fly the maiden back to the pirate.'

'I'll remember that,' Carly had said.

Now she closed her fingers round the little carving and thought, I'll give it away. Not to William, I don't want to keep on seeing it. But I'll go on remembering it, and everything else that has happened these past two weeks. If I could fly back to him I would. Again and again, to wherever he is.

Her fingers opened again and she stared at the little lion. I love Liam, she thought. As well as the chemistry, the sexual attraction, I love his strength, his mind, the way he can make me angry and make me laugh. I want to run to him instead of holding back. I want him to say that he's had a lousy day but that everything's all right now because he's with me.

Liam had never really needed anyone, Madame Corbé had said, but Liam had thought that Carly was a girl for whom a man might do most things, short of murder. He'd changed his mind slightly since he'd known her better. He no longer thought she was all that dangerous—to Roland maybe but not to him. But he still found her attractive and they would be meeting in England arranging business matters. Small fry to him, but she would see that he kept involved. And tomorrow, Roland wouldn't want to spend several hours taking her to the airport, but perhaps she could say to Liam, 'I've been thinking, I think it might be better after all if you took me to Dinard. If you don't mind.'

She put the lion back in the case and took a few steps towards the door. 'I'm sorry I said the things you heard me saying,' she could tell him—if she could catch him. 'I didn't mean them, I was upset and I lost my head, and I said that I hoped I'd never set eyes on you again when we get back home, but if I don't it will be like going through the rest of my life in the dark.'

She stopped before she opened the door, twisting her hands together, biting her lip. She couldn't say that, but it was true, and she was filled with self-doubts, suddenly and painfully unsure of herself. She had never thought this could happen to her, that one man could matter so much that she was scared to death and didn't know what to do.

It was no good planning a thing. She couldn't go out and follow him because she wouldn't know what to say. She had to give herself time to adapt, because right now she could only whisper, 'I love him,' until she wasn't surprised by it any more. If she could get used to it, and accept it, then perhaps the tongue-tied shyness would go and she could act naturally and use all the seductiveness she could muster without anyone guessing that the man she smiled at had become the centre of her world.

Visitors were coming this evening. It was Carly's goodbye dinner party. She had left the bronze dress hanging in the closet and she put a few more things in the case, then took off her dress and jacket and swallowed a couple of aspirins, and slipped into the sheets of Napoleon's bed. The nerves and muscles at the back of her neck and skull were beginning to tighten, and there was a risk of a nervous headache unless she relaxed. So she took the aspirins and waited for sleep.

She woke in plenty of time and lay still for a moment

or two, then moved cautiously as though she had been badly shaken up before she slept and was testing for pain. Falling in love with Liam was the most traumatic thing that had ever happened to her. It could break her, but it had happened, she couldn't stop it now, so she put on the bronze dress, and clasped on the gilt bracelets, excited and scared.

It was a very long time since Carly had been so vulnerable. That was why she had panicked when Madame Corbé had started talking of marriage and Liam. Because his emphatic rejection and cold amusement would have cut her to the heart.

She stood back, to get the best view she could in the small mirror, and hoped she looked all right. Her customary confidence was at a low ebb tonight, and when she passed one of the maids at the top of the stairs and Renée admired the shining dress, '*Ah, très jolie!*' Carly said gratefully, '*Merci, vous êtes gentille.*'

Down in the hall she saw Roland through the open door of the room that was used as an office, and tapped and asked, 'May I have a word?'

She had some idea of trying to make peace. It was impulsive and from his expression unlikely to do much good. He looked up from a list he seemed to be checking and frowned, and she said, 'Sorry about this afternoon,' but before she could go on, 'You don't really want to marry me, but it wasn't true what Liam said,' Roland burst out,

'Why apologise? Most women prefer womanisers.'

'Look, I——'

'No harm done,' said Roland curtly. 'I'm glad you enjoyed yourself, but it's as well you're leaving tomorrow as Alison Parry's arriving the day after.'

Carly felt real pain stab through her. While she was

here Liam had had phone calls. Women looked at him, and brightened when he looked at them, he had that kind of charisma, but hearing that Alison would be waiting when he came back from seeing Carly on to her plane was like a door slammed in her face. This was rejection. This told her he had no need of her.

'Although you could have stayed on,' said Roland, still smarting and taking his revenge. 'She wouldn't have wanted your room. She's sharing Liam's.'

Carly went into the drawing room where Madame Corbé was listening to music and waiting for her guests. Carly went straight to her, and she smiled and said, 'I looked into your room earlier, my dear. You were resting.'

'I took some headache pills,' Carly explained, 'and went to sleep for a while.'

'Oh dear, I am sorry.' Madame peered closer. 'How is the headache?'

'Quite gone.' This was a different agony, worse than a blinding migraine, although she could finish with one of those too before the evening ended. She wished now that she hadn't come down, or that she hadn't said the headache was better, then she would have had an excuse to return to her room before long.

As it was she had to sit out, and she had a wretched time. She had met all the guests before, and they greeted her like a friend and her face was stiff with smiling. As soon as he arrived the doctor made a show of asking Madame Corbé how she was feeling, and she said very well and grimaced slightly and he chuckled, looking first at her and then across at Liam.

Carly didn't follow his glance. She was afraid that if she looked at Liam her eyes would give her away. She tried to pretend he wasn't there, looking everywhere else, listening to the conversation which was part-English, part-French. She could more or less follow the French after a fortnight's practice, and she ate the delicious meal and drank several glasses of wine and tried to look happy and animated.

When Liam spoke she concentrated on her plate, and wished she could clap her hands over her ears because the sound of his voice made her ache inside, but everyone else seemed to be having a pleasant evening.

Especially a girl called Véronique, who was seated by Roland and with whom he flirted all through the meal. She dug into her purse to bring out her diary and see if she was free for two evenings next week, and decided she was so that Roland fixed up a concert somewhere and dinner somewhere else, and that made Carly smile.

Roland's ego was being restored. Carly had turned him down, but he was showing her that an even prettier girl fancied him. Her family ran the strawberry farm and she had strawberry blonde hair, a peaches and cream complexion, and looked adoringly at Roland.

Maybe it will be you, thought Carly, and rather hoped it would. Then she thought about Alison Parry with her cloud of fair hair spread out over Liam's pillow, and jealousy burned inside her rising into the back of her throat like acid so that she could eat no more.

It was late when they went. They all said goodbye to Carly and hoped to see her again, and Madame Corbé said she would be bringing a small friend next time, and Carly thought, poor William, you would have loved it here, but at least you'll never know you were invited.

She only wanted to get to her room now and away in the morning. She would never come back, but she smiled all through the goodbyes and said, 'If any of you are ever in England——' and wondered what they would make of Ruth's home after this.

Perhaps she would move in with Barney, and show Liam as Roland was showing her that there were plenty more pebbles in the sea. She wouldn't, of course. She might be mixing her metaphors, but she knew with a clear inner certainty that for her there was only loneliness ahead.

She had hoped the wine might help, but all it had done was blur a few edges, and she breathed in the night air deeply as she stood at the top of the steps with Madame Corbé, watching the men directing the cars out. Roland called, '*A lundi*,' presumably after Véronique, and as Liam came back Carly went into the house.

Roland must have followed Liam because Madame Corbé said, 'Véronique is a very sweet girl,' and Roland agreed, 'She certainly is.'

'Do you mind if I say goodnight?' said Carly. 'It's been a lovely evening.'

Madame kissed her cheek, and Carly smiled at Roland and said, 'I think you're right, Véronique is sweet.' She managed to answer Liam's goodnight without looking at him—it was childish, but she could not face him—and she left them in the hall and went to her room, to gather up a nightdress and get ready for bed.

In the bathroom, having stripped off her clothes and her make-up, she splashed cold water on her face, although she might have fallen asleep easier if she hadn't sobered herself. There was no one in the corridor, but her bedroom door was ajar. She was almost sure she hadn't left it like that ten minutes ago, and she stepped in warily, eyes darting, and as she reached for the switch she saw him standing at the window and her hand fell.

He was just a shadow, something tall and dark, not even moving, but she knew who it was before he said,

'You're taking Véronique in good part. She's very suitable, but it's nice to know you agree she's sweet.'

Carly was carrying clothes and toilet bag and she clutched them to her, and heard her voice like somebody else's saying, 'She looks good enough to eat. Pour cream over her and you'd have a fruit salad.'

'You shouldn't have had that fourth glass,' said Liam, but she was sober and how dared he come in here? What was he doing now? Why couldn't he leave her in peace and stop hounding her?

'You were *counting*?' she shrilled. 'Still watching me? Why are you still watching me?'

'Because I can't keep my eyes off you.' His voice was rough. 'Why haven't you looked at me once all night?' He was moving to a light switch and Carly croaked,

'Don't put the light on!' All she wore was a thin nightdress, but it wasn't that. She didn't want him to see her eyes, and she closed them tightly as though the electric light could burn and blind her.

Liam didn't switch it on. He reached her in darkness, catching her wrist, and she dropped the things she was carrying and they almost tripped her up as he drew her towards the window.

Moonlight was there. 'Look at me,' he said.

He loosed her wrist and cupped her face so that she had to look up at him, and she strained against his touch, panting, 'What for? Why do you care whether I look at you or not? Perhaps I don't want to look at you!'

His nearness was destroying her. The longing for him was in her blood and her bones, and when he turned from her she almost cried out.

He moved a little way, a silhouette, arms folded, she thought, and said, 'I had no right to say we were lovers. It was inexcusable, but my only excuse is that at the time it seemed the truth.' It had seemed the truth to her too, when they walked through that market square, fingers entwined. As though she had gone into his arms many times, giving herself over to the tenderness of his hands with such a rapture of passion. 'I couldn't let you marry him,' Liam said slowly, and she grated,

'Don't tell me that again!' That he feared for Roland because Gerald Collett had ended in jail. But she had no power. She was weak as water. Liam wanted her, that was why he was here, and once he started to make love to her she would have no defences because she wanted him. But the power would be his and never hers, because she was the one in love.

She stumbled across the room asking shakily, 'And what do you think I might have done to Roland? Killed him?'

'Not you,' said Liam. 'Me.' Carly reached for support and held on to one of the carved bedposts and he went on, very quietly, 'I changed my mind about you since I met you again. I don't know exactly when, but I do know I've no reservations now. I'd murder for you. I knew Roland had never been to your room, nor you to his. I've slept with my door open, no one would have got past me.'

She spoke in a whisper through rigid lips. 'He told me your film star was coming next week—Alison Parry. Sharing your room.'

'No.' Perhaps Roland had lied. Perhaps he had overheard a phone call and misunderstood. 'The 'no' was decisive. 'I won't be here next week,' said Liam. 'You can't ask Roland to drive you tomorrow. I'll take you, and we'll stop at Lonfleur.'

The little town. Carly gave a strangled cry and Liam said quickly, 'Let me say it all first. Then we'll talk, argue if you like, but let me tell you how it is with me.

'I want to go back there with you because it was so right there. As though wherever we went we would come back from time to time. The house that was for sale. Do you remember it?'

'I remember,' she breathed into the darkness.

'I phoned the agents and said I wanted to look at it. The key's waiting. I wanted to walk through it with you. If you liked it I'd buy it. We could stay there for the week, I thought. A hotel, or even in the house—it could be arranged. I wanted to ask you——'

Perhaps it was the four glasses of wine, but she was hearing voices, dreaming dreams. Liam wasn't really over there, saying incredible things in a quiet controlled voice. Then suddenly the voice changed and became ragged and harsh like a man under torture. 'What I heard you shouting, was that what you really felt, that the idea of marrying me was obscene?'

'No, oh *no* . . .' Carly had been gripping the bedpost with both hands so hard that the carving was cutting. She thought wildly, my legs won't carry me, if I let go I shall fall, and she whispered, 'Please come here.'

But she held her arms wide and when Liam reached her she fell against him and he said huskily, 'May I kiss you?'

'Kiss me?' She could feel his breath on her lips. 'That isn't much to ask.'

'But I can't promise when the kissing would stop.'

She laughed softly, 'I suppose I can always say— enough.'

He put an arm around her, a hand over a breast, and kissed her gently, slowly, savouring her lips, while her heartbeats quickened until the darkness whirled around her and she was falling on to the soft coverlet of Napoleon's bed, still in Liam's arms, and she knew that she could never say stop.

Harlequin Plus

A WORD ABOUT THE AUTHOR

Jane Donnelly was born and raised in England.
Trained as a journalist, she worked as a reporter
on the local newspaper in a village on the edge of
the Cotswolds, not far from Birmingham. After
the birth of her daughter, she became the
television critic for the *Birmingham Gazette*.

She was widowed when her daughter was only
five and moved from her beloved village to
Lancashire in the north. It was there that she
began to write fiction—short stories, thrillers
and movie scripts. When her daughter was in her
teens, Jane attempted her first full-length book.
She loved the experience—and so did her
publisher—and continues to write warmhearted
romances ... almost fifteen years after the pub-
lication of *A Man Apart* (Romance #1227).

Jane returned to her former home in the
Cotswolds when she learned that a certain
historic house, a picture-perfect setting for
writers, was for sale. She believes that her
"cottage" is under some sort of happy magical
spell. "After all," she says, "animals immediately
make themselves at home here, and in the garden
everything grows lushly!"

4 FREE
Harlequin Romances

Get all the latest books before they're sold out!

As a Harlequin subscriber you actually receive your personal copies of the latest Romances immediately after they come off the press, so you're sure of getting all 6 each month.

Cancel your subscription whenever you wish!

You don't have to buy any minimum number of books. Whenever you decide to stop your subscription just let us know and we'll cancel all further shipments.

Your FREE gift includes

- *Anne Hampson* — Beyond the Sweet Waters
- *Anne Mather* — The Arrogant Duke
- *Violet Winspear* — Cap Flamingo
- *Nerina Hilliard* — Teachers Must Learn